SHORT STORY 10-PACK

MICHAEL KINGSWOOD

CONTENTS

About This Book   v

Lords of the Remnant   1
How NOT To Rescue A Damsel in Distress   13
The Blob On The Rock   21
Falling Softly   39
The Memory Of Justice   49
Measuring Up   59
A Chat Before Dinner   73
First Blood   81
Who Ate My Sock?   93
Brother In Law, Brother In Blood   101

Message From The Author   113
Mailing List   115
Supporting Patronage   117
About The Author   119
More Books By Michael Kingswood   121

ABOUT THIS BOOK

A desperate struggle against an alien invasion.

A rescue attempt that goes haywire.

A scientific expedition endangered by its own discovery.

An assassin's most lucrative job, and also his most dangerous.

A victim's search for true justice. Or is it just revenge?

A young soldier learning the ropes.

A zombie's rant about the difficulties of his life.

A scout's first combat mission.

A missing sock leads to a terrifying discovery.

A betrothed's love runs up against a brother's protectiveness.

ABOUT THIS BOOK

Short Story 10-Pack is a collection of ten engrossing short stories from science fiction/fantasy author Michael Kingswood

---

Enjoy the book! After you're done, please come to Michael's website and sign up for his mailing list at www.michaelkingswood.com/newsletter-signup/. Guaranteed to be spam free, he uses it to announce new releases and special promotions for his fans.

LORDS OF THE REMNANT

They came at dawn, a streaming mass of bodies falling from the sky. As with everything else about them, this method of attack took us completely by surprise, and we had no immediate defense against it.

It was as though we were half a step behind them each time we met.

When the Centauri colony reported contact with craft of unknown origin, the people living in the various settlements in the Sol system were amazed, excited, filled with joy.

We were no longer alone! It was real, and undeniable.

Two weeks later, when the next transmission from Centauri brought news of the opening of hostilities, that feeling of euphoria changed to one of dread.

Mankind had stopped warring with itself centuries ago. With the exception of certain outlaw elements, the average person had no concept of war, or how to fight one. Yes, there were old warships drydocked in a station orbiting at the trans-lunar LaGrange point, near the James Webb historical site, but it had been decades since the reserve units charged with their mainte-nance had even powered them up.

All at once, though, those relics of man's warlike past became the Sol system's only hope of defense, and every available resource was put to making the small armada ready for action. But as further transmissions arrived from Centauri, we all began to realize that thirty ships, crewed by people with no experience in battle, would be of little use against the invaders if they came to Sol next.

And so Congress voted to build planetary defense grids on Earth, Mars, Luna, Europa, and Titan. The theory was that if we built large automated weapons arrays, the planets would be impregnable against any vessels that managed to make it past our small battle fleet.

The problem was time.

Centauri was about four light years away. At our best cruising speeds, it was a trip of about ten earth years, and that was damn little time to build the kinds of systems the plans called for.

But the continuing transmissions from Centauri provided all the motivation we needed. Pictures of the aliens' relentless advance, and our kinsmen's inevitable defeat, spurred every industry to put aside everything except war preparations.

When, two years after the first one, the final transmission from Centauri came through, a static-laced image of a man with hopeless, yet undefeated eyes bidding farewell to the rest of us, we figured we had at a minimum another five or six years to prepare. The aliens would want to take time to lick their wounds, consolidate their holdings, before they moved on, wouldn't they?

They arrived a month later.

How they managed it, even our greatest scientists could not explain. It meant they'd travelled so close to the speed of light that there was no point in measuring the difference. Assuming they'd left Centauri immediately after the final battle. If they'd lingered at all to regroup...well, that meant the impossible: they'd travelled faster than light to reach Sol, and that could not be.

Could it?

Titan and Europa were overrun almost immediately. Their

defense grids were only just being started, and their small populations were ill-prepared to fight off the aliens' assault.

Our small armada met the alien fleet between Mars and Jupiter. They put up a good struggle, but in the end they were outnumbered and outgunned. With our fleet gone, the aliens advanced on the Mars colonies.

They held out a lot longer. Many of us on Earth and Luna wanted to send forces to assist the colonies in resisting the attack. We thought that if we joined humanity's forces in one place, we had a decent chance of beating them back.

But "wiser" heads prevailed, and the powers that be determined to instead focus on building up the Terran defense grid. In the year it took for Mars to fall, we built an impressive array of particle beam cannons, EMP transmitters, orbital minefields, and numerous other devices designed to ward off the alien fleet.

But when it came to be our turn, the invaders did not oblige us. Their fleet stood off, well beyond Luna's orbit, and did nothing.

Or so we thought.

Late last night, satellite observation posts detected small bursts of energy from the alien ships.

At first, we didn't know what was going on. But then, just a couple hours ago, low earth orbit weather analysis satellites detected thousands upon thousands of small objects approaching re-entry interface. Our defense grid, designed to target and take out the aliens' large battleships, never even noticed the multitude of man-sized craft until it was too late.

The civil defense sirens went off at five o'clock local time, rousing the populace, those who'd been able to sleep at all, in time to see the last of the plasma trails burn out as the aliens completed re-entry and plunged through the air toward the ground.

I had the midwatch in the civil defense station on the south side of town. When the report came in, I suggested we not sound the sirens at all. Better to not panic people.

After all, wouldn't dying in your sleep be preferable to living in desperate fear for a few hours before the end?

Of course, that was easy for me to say, as my Lieutenant kindly pointed out. The schmuck actually gave a speech about how we were going to beat these alien bastards back. We were going to whip their asses, you understand.

I managed to suppress a sarcastic reply, but I'm sure he saw my smirk. But what was we he going to do, write me up? We needed every swinging dick who could hold a rifle out in the field, and he knew it.

So that's how I found myself at the outskirts of the forest southeast of town, watching the tens of thousands of tiny black specks that I knew were alien shock troops grow larger and larger in the sky. I looked left and right at the other guys in my platoon and wondered, for the hundredth time, what the hell we were doing.

There were maybe a couple hundred of us, total. There was no way we'd be able to hold them on our own. Headquarters had promised help was on the way as soon as it could get here from the staging area a hundred clicks west, but the aliens were dropping in all over the world, from what I could tell.

It would be way past lucky if they didn't drop on the staging area as well.

Then there was no time to think about it. The first of the invading troopers flared, metallic wings similar to a butterfly's extending from its metallic re-entry suit, and settled onto the ground maybe half a kilometer ahead of our lines.

No one had to give the order to fire. A hundred Particle Rifles, smaller cousins of the particle beam cannons in orbit around the Earth, fired nearly in unison, and the first alien disappeared in a superheated fireball.

But a second landed. Then a third. A fifth. A twentieth. A hundredth.

We dispatched the first hundred or so easily enough. They landed far enough apart that we were able to concentrate our fire to take them out quickly. But after that, they began landing in groups of ten or twenty, and it was all we could do to hold our ground. The invaders fell by the dozen as we fell back, but for every one that fell, ten landed behind it as replacements.

And they began to return fire.

Their weapons did not spew the same supercharged ions that ours did. They were smaller, less intimidating to look at, but far more precise and deadly. My best buddy in the platoon shrieked and literally melted next to me, his body dissolving into a disgusting, amorphous goo when the beam from an invader's weapon struck him, never mind the phasing body armor he wore.

I took down the alien who got him, but the sight of him dying that way freaked me out more than anything I'd ever seen.

I knew, when my number got called in the selection six months prior, that I was not going to live to see the end of the war. We all did, though we never talked about it, and tried not to think about it. But as we went through our drills, learning how to use our weapons and armor, each of us knew it was futile.

We were all doomed.

Well, maybe not all of us realized it. The Lieutenant, that silly bastard, seemed to really believe we could prevail. So did a few other guys in the unit. But from the get-go, I knew we were on a fool's errand.

So I decided to live it up in the time I had left. Lord knew there were girls aplenty waiting in line to give it up to a soldier, and who was I to deny them their fantasies? It was every man's dream for a while there, and I almost forgot about the fate awaiting me.

Awaiting us all.

I surely never thought it would come for us so soon. Or that we would die such gruesome deaths.

Another buddy getting liquified next to me drew me back to the present, and I hit the dirt behind a fallen tree. Three separate alien beams traced through the air where I'd just been standing, and I breathed a sigh of relief that my reflexes were as quick as they were.

Glancing left and right, I could see two or three other guys from my unit, crouching behind cover as I was. Where was everyone else?

My earbud, tuned to the command circuit, carried the Lieutenant's voice. It sounded like he was beginning to order a withdrawal, but his words turned into an agonized, horrified screech, then all that came through the earbud was static.

The other men on either side of me panicked as the chain of command broke down. One by one, they scrambled backwards, away from the advancing aliens.

And one by one they were struck down, alien beams hitting them the instant they emerged from cover.

It took a minute for me to realize that I was completely alone.

Alien invaders streamed past my position on either side. They apparently didn't realize I was there, and still kicking. For a heartbeat the thought passed through my head that I could make it if I just played dead.

Then a surge of anger, outrage even, filled me.

I can't tell you now why I did it, or how. I don't remember actually deciding to do it, or telling my legs to. Before I even realized it, I found myself standing upright, turning my rifle on alien after alien, incinerating an invader with each shot.

On and on I shot, raking my fire from left to right.

I relished every invader's scream as it went down, every flash of fire as my rounds struck home. I was going down, but by God, I'd take as many of them with me as I could.

Then the rifle stopped firing. I'd used up the entire ammo receiver. I reached for a replacement, but found my belt pouches empty.

I must have reloaded and fired through them all without realizing it.

All around me, the battlefield was obscured with smoke. Everywhere I looked, all I could see were craters, the shattered remains of alien invaders, and smoke rising from both. There must have been a hundred of the bastards lying dead or mortally wounded in my immediate vicinity.

For a moment, I actually thought I'd won.

Then a gust of wind thinned out the smoke, revealing the massed multitudes of invaders, gathered in a half-circle around me, watching.

Waiting.

I was done.

Fine, if that's how it was going to be, I wasn't going to give the bastards the satisfaction of watching me run.

With a roar, I threw my rifle at the closest of them and drew my bowie knife. Then I charged.

A single invader, armored differently from the others, raised its weapon toward me as I advanced. I knew it would get me before I could do anything with my knife, so I threw the blade at it.

The alien fired as I threw.

It felt like a ball-peen hammer slugged me in the chest, and I fell over. I had only a heartbeat to wonder why I wasn't melting before I lost consciousness.

I couldn't tell you how long I was out, but when I came to, I found myself in a large oval-shaped room. The walls were painted a light cream color. The ceiling was plain, unadorned except for recessed lighting panels. I was resting on a mattress, or couch, of come sort.

And I was no longer in my body armor. Instead, I wore a loose-fitting grey robe, almost like a hospital gown.

It was hard to move, but I managed to sit up after a few moments of trying. The rest of the room came into view as I did, and my jaw dropped. One side of the room was dominated by a window looking out into space.

I knew it was space, because I could see Luna not far off, and past it, Earth. I'd never been off world before. The view was awe-inspiring, and for a moment, the implication of what I was seeing was lost on me.

"It's quite a view, isn't it?"

The voice surprised me for two reasons. One, I hadn't noticed any other people in the room with me. Two, it spoke perfect english, and in a North American accent.

I looked around for the source of the voice, and beheld a man in his middle years sitting in an armchair not far from me. He had dark brown hair, nearly black, and sharp hazel eyes. His nose was romanesque, and he had large, protruding ears.

I did a double-take.

His ears were not just large, they were huge. And pointed. For that matter, his eyes were not human either: instead of round, his irises were slits, like a cat's.

The alien smirked ever so slightly as I drew back from him. "Believe me, you people look just as strange to us as we do to you."

"How..." I swallowed. "How do you - ?"

"Know your language?" Again, the alien smirked. "If you know the enemy and know yourself, you need not fear the result of a hundred battles."

That phrase seemed familiar somehow, but I couldn't put my finger on it. "I've heard that before," I said, almost to myself.

The alien nodded. "I should hope so. We spent many years training the man you know as Sun Tzu. He never knew it of course."

"You...trained him?" I knew I sounded incredulous. And, well, I was.

"Of course. We make it our business to help the younger species grow, become strong."

This was all coming a bit too fast. Processing what the alien was saying, on top of getting my mind around being alive and on an alien ship was beginning to make my head hurt.

I couldn't find the right words to say, so I settled for shaking my head.

The alien touched something on the arm of his chair, and the wall opposite the window to space flickered, then displayed a series of images. Humans, in all states of dress that obviously spanned history, engaged in battle after battle. The graphic bloodshed made me wince, but the alien only smiled as he watched the stream of images.

"Almost from the beginning, you showed promise. You were strong, resourceful, adaptive. You just needed...prodding...to get you moving down the path to greatness."

More images flashed up on the screen, this time of individuals. Caesar. Genghis Kahn. Sun Tzu. Saladin. Napoleon. Nelson. Kaiser Wilhelm. Hitler. MacArthur. Abu Nadal. Gorshkov. Li Sung. Mendoza. The greatest military leaders in human history streamed past in an unbroken line until, after Thorton, the list abruptly ended.

"We influenced the greatest among you, helped them become better. Without their knowing, of course. And they led you to the height of your strength." He sighed before continuing. "As you can imagine, we were gravely disappointed when you decided to turn away from the path of greatness." The alien shook his head in disapproval.

"No we haven't. We live among the stars now, in peace - "

"Peace!" The alien spat the word like a curse as he turned to give me his full attention again. His features contorted in a grimace of disgust. "Yes, you've lived in peace. And stagnated."

He gestured toward the wall again, where a new image appeared.

This one was video. It only took a second for me to realize I was looking at a live feed from Earth's surface. Bile rose in my stomach as I watched women, children, the elderly, the wounded, and the fearful fleeing before the advancing alien forces.

But they didn't make it far. They fell by the dozen as the aliens fired into the fleeing crowd. There was no audio, but I could imagine their terrified, despairing screams as they sought in vain to escape their fate.

"Look at them," said the alien, contempt in his voice. "Weak. Pathetic. Not one of them has the will to fight for his own survival. Instead, they made themselves sheep for the slaughter." He shook his head again.

"They're unarmed and without training. If - "

"Weapons are nothing. Training is nothing." The alien tapped the side of his head with his index finger and continued. "Will is everything. The will to not give in. To struggle and overcome, to fight. Show me a coward with training against a person of will who never thought of how to fight, and the willful person will win three times out of four." He leaned toward me, fixing me with his strange gaze. "How many were in your town, and how many of you came out to fight against us? You have more than enough numbers to beat us if you had the will to try. You see the result of your species' cowardice there."

"I don't understand. You *want* us to fight?"

"Of course. Conflict is the driving force behind growth, behind evolution. A species that stops fighting stops improving itself. It stagnates, as you have. We thought that you had grown enough to not need further prodding, but the last several hundred of your years showed us that the maturity to accept the most basic facts of existence still eludes you. And so we have come again, to teach you a lesson you should never have forgotten: to live without conflict is to tread upon the path to oblivion."

I sank back onto the couch, stunned.

The alien's matter-of-fact speech was proof enough that what he said was the truth. All this time, mankind had patted itself on the back for finally finding a way to live at peace with itself, and all the while that very peace was setting us up for extermination.

But if that were so, why...

"Why are you telling me this? For that matter, why am I even alive?"

"Because you have a fighter's spirit." The alien stood and walked over to me. "If your species is to return to greatness, its new leaders must be of the correct temperament. Of all your comrades on the battlefield, only you had the will to fight to the end. That kind of will is exactly what is needed."

I shook my head in denial. "I just got angry."

"And your anger gave you strength." The alien gestured for me to stand up, and I complied, slowly. I was pretty sure I knew what the alien had in mind, but decided to hear him out, anyway.

Rather that speaking, though, he gestured toward the window, and I looked out.

Down on earth, I could see, even from this distance out in space, flashes of explosions in several locations around the globe. They must have detonated some truly massive bombs for us to be able to see them from way out here. We stood there for what seemed a long time, just watching the fireworks.

Finally, the alien spoke again.

"As you can see, if we wished to, we could eliminate your species completely. But we believe you still have promise, so we're giving mankind a fresh start. We will spare a remnant, enough to rebuild in a reasonable amount of time. You will help to lead that remnant on the proper path."

"I'll not be your stooge."

The alien chuckled. "And so you won't. After this is done, you'll never see me or mine again. But we'll be watching, helping, prodding, just as we always have. And hoping that this time, you'll get it right."

"And if I say no?"

The alien was silent for a moment, and I glanced sidelong at him. Rather than looking at me, his gaze remained fixed on Earth. When he finally spoke, his voice carried a hard edge.

"You may refuse, and we'll simply set you back on Earth. You might even survive to be one of the remnant. But I promise you, life will be less than pleasant. We'll see to that. You'll wish very quickly that you'd accepted our offer."

Turning away from the window, the alien walked back to his chair and touched the arm rest again. Part of the wall near the display screen opened, and a group of people walked in.

They numbered about twenty or thirty, and were all human. Male, female, dark, light, tall, short, slim, muscular, but none fat, they represented all the sub-races of humanity. Leading them was a tall, muscular man with a proud face and hard eyes. It took me a moment to realize where I recognized him from: he was the man in the last transmission from Centauri.

The group stopped when they reached the alien's chair and turned their eyes on me. I felt laid bare, naked, beneath their collective gaze.

"Decide now," said the alien. "Will you join these others as a Lord of the remnant, and lead mankind back to greatness, or will you refuse, and take your chances with those on the world below?"

I looked from the alien to the Centauri man's face, then down the line of humans to the last, a lovely young lady of Czech decent, unless I missed my guess.

Next, I turned and looked out the window, toward the besieged Earth.

It was not a hard decision to make.

HOW NOT TO RESCUE A DAMSEL IN DISTRESS

L arian awoke to find himself dangling by his wrists from a ring in the ceiling. He could just barely touch the floor with his tiptoes. Not quite enough to relieve the pressure on his wrists. The rope that bound them was rough; already he could tell his wrists were rubbed raw. Things had most certainly NOT gone according to plan.

Freshly graduated from the Martial Academy in Tel Cerelon, he returned home on leave to see his friends and family...and his girl...one last time before heading off to the front.

There was a war on, sure, but the General Staff was reasonable about those sorts of things. Some argued it was foolish to allow recruits leave so soon. The Mar Tabban would never do such a thing. But then, isn't that why they were fighting in the first place?

Larian was excited to get out to the war, but he was still glad for the chance to say goodbye. To say he was disappointed and angered when he arrived home to find his father barely holding on to life from a sword cut and his girl kidnapped by brigands would be a vast understatement.

When he learned the details of what happened, he strapped on his armor, belted on his sword, and set out after the brigands. Several of his friends tried to talk him out of it. The brigands were too strong. He was going to get himself killed. Rosaline would be dead or sold to flesh peddlers by the time he caught up to them.

But he would hear none of it. He was a trained soldier, the best swordsman in his recruit class, and these rabble would feel his wrath, by heaven!

He never stopped to think that he was just one man against a dozen. Or that some of those dozen may have been as well trained as he, that some may have been army deserters. Or that they had more experience in laying ambushes and tracking than he.

It was with almost laughable ease that he fell into the brigands' trap as he approached Jergan's Peak. One moment he was following the faint trail of their passing, and the next he felt a hard tug on his ankle and found himself hoisted up into the air. Taken by a simple lasso booby-trap!

He didn't have time to curse his stupidity, as the brigands emerged from the underbrush and set upon him. Though upside down, he was far from helpless. He managed to gut one of them before the others got his sword away and bound him fully.

"Freshly-minted soldier boy trying to play hero, eh?" mocked the brigands' leader after the dust settled. "I bet you came for this, didn't you?"

He tugged on a rope in his hand, and Rosaline came stumbling out from behind a nearby tree. Her hands were bound behind her back and she wore a collar around her neck, which was attached to the rope in the leader's hand.

Anger blotted out fear in Larian's mind when he beheld his girl in that state. "Let her go, you bastards!" he growled.

The leader laughed in his face.

"Let a choice piece of ass like this go? Because you say so? Not a chance."

Pulling Rosaline closer, he made a point of fondling her and gave Larian a lecherous wink. "I think I'll keep you alive so you can watch me show her a good time or two. Before I do you like you did Rudrick."

To his henchmen, he ordered, "Drug him!"

Larian struggled as best he could, but the brigands had little trouble forcing a potion of some sort down his throat. Before long, his head started to spin and he dropped into unconsciousness.

So here he was. Some hero.

The worst part was that he'd be declared a deserter when he didn't return from leave. Not only would he be dead, but his family's name would be tarnished forever. It just wasn't fair.

Frustration, fear, and despair all welled up in his mind, and he felt tears begin to form in his eyes. Blast it! He was supposed to be a soldier. A man! He needed to get ahold of himself. There were plenty of stories about fellows getting out of worse fixes than this.

He looked around the room, trying to find some way to free himself.

In reality, room was probably a misnomer. He was in a small hollow of rock, maybe five feet across and five deep, with an opening leading to a larger rock chamber in front of him. It appeared he was in a cave complex.

He didn't see any guards, but there was a flickering light to the left, and he heard a couple voices engaged in conversation. More light came from overhead as well. Looking up, Larian could see a narrow shaft that allowed sunlight into the chamber. If he could just get to that shaft somehow, it looked like an easy climb.

The voices became louder, and a moment later two rough-looking men stepped into view. Both wore thick leather armor and had broad-bladed swords on their hips. Numerous scars crisscrossed the older man's face. The younger was actually fairly well groomed, with strong features that Larian supposed a lady might find appealing.

Seeing him awake, the older man emitted a nasty little giggle and nudged his comrade with his elbow.

"Oh good. Keep an eye on him, and I'll let Wellis know he's ready for the first session."

With that, scarface turned and hurried off.

The younger brigand frowned slightly. "Better for you if you'd not awakened, friend. For what it's worth, I'm sorry for what's about to happen. Robbing a man, or killing him in a fair fight is one thing. But this..." He shook his head slowly. "Not my thing." Was the brigand actually looking at him with pity?

"Well, you could just let me go, if it bothers you so much. You could say I managed to wriggle free and got the better of you."

The brigand looked at him like he was nuts. "I'm not that sorry. It's my ass if....Aggghhhh!"

Larian was amazed to see the tip of a sword emerge from the front of the brigand's chest. The brigand choked and spluttered for a moment, clutching in vain at the blade, then his knees buckled and he slid off the blade and to the floor, dead.

Rosaline stood behind him, Larian's now bloody blade in her hands and a fierce light in her eyes.

"Rosaline??? How did..."

She raised a finger to her lips, and he shut up. Moving quickly, she ducked out of sight, then returned a moment later with a stool, which she set on the ground in front of Larian. Setting his sword down and pulling a knife from behind her belt, she stood up on the stool and set to work cutting the rope. As she cut, she spoke, her voice barely above a whisper.

"The guy they had guarding me kept ogling, so I convinced him I would let him...well, you know." She flushed red in her cheeks, but her lovely face remained determined and focused. "He kissed me, and I unbuckled his belt and pulled down his pants. Of course he didn't think of anything but what he wanted, so he didn't notice I had his knife until I gelded him."

Larian felt a sympathetic pain in his gut. True, these brigands were scum, but still, that was just harsh. Wait a minute. "What do you mean, you kissed him?"

Rosaline gave him a level look. "Focus, Larian. Do you want to get out of here or not?"

"Yes, definitely."

"Then shut up. I've almost got it." She began sawing at the rope more briskly, and Larian could feel the knot begin to loosen. Hope, so close to gone a moment before, surged within him. They were going to get out of this after all! Then, he heard voices. Several of them, and getting nearer.

"Hurry, Ros. They're coming. Oww!"

The last strand of the rope parted beneath Rosaline's knife, but before she could stop her cut, the knife also bit deeply into the flesh of Larian's right hand.

The sudden release of the rope came as much a surprise as the cut to his hand, and he dropped to his knees before he was able to catch himself. He bumped Rosaline as he fell, and she tumbled to the floor also. They had barely begun to extricate themselves when three brigands rounded the corner, the leader in front.

"Here, what's this then?" The leader took in the situation at a glance, his scowl deepening when he saw his fallen man. "You'll be a long time in dying. The both of you." Over his shoulder, he barked "Kolin! Gil!"

The two fellows with him, one of them Larian's old friend scar-face, drew steel and moved forward.

Larian moved frantically to his feet, grabbing up his sword from where Rosaline dropped it. His right hand was covered in blood, but he had no time to wipe it off or to stem the flow before the brigands were on them.

He parried a cut from the first brigand and nearly lost his grip during his riposte when the blade twisted in his grip. As a result, the flat of the blade struck the brigand on his cheek, so what would have been a killing blow merely sent the fellow reeling into his comrade.

In the brief respite that followed, Larian wiped his hand on his shirt and look a firmer grip, readying himself for a second pass.

But it turned out to be unnecessary. Rosaline leaped onto the brigands while they were still tangled together, her knife darting to take the first in the throat and the second in the chest. Both looked unbelieving as they fell, stricken by a petite female. The brigand leader was stunned as well. Eyes wide, he looked from the two dead men to Rosaline and back for a moment. Then he laughed, a throaty guffaw that echoed through the cave chamber.

"The kitten has claws! I'm going to enjoy this."

He moved so quickly, drawing and attacking in one fluid motion, that Larian didn't realize the brigand leader's sword was out of its scabbard until it was almost to his throat.

Only a desperate upward parry and a leap backward saved his life, but his back slammed into the cave wall, and he lost his breath for a moment.

The leader advanced, sensing Larian's disorientation, but again Rosaline saved him. She came at the leader from the side, her knife stabbed at his kidney.

He didn't even look away from Larian as he removed his left hand from the grip of his sword and grabbed Rosaline's knife-hand in mid-stab. She blinked in surprise, then squealed in pain when the leader turned his hand over and pressed up, putting her into a wrist-lock that forced her up onto her toes.

Larian heard the clink of her knife hitting the stone floor as he pushed himself off the wall. He attacked, a low cut that stopped midway and became a rising thrust toward the leader's sternum.

But he was unsuccessful again.

The leader executed some kind of spiraling parry that Larian had never seen before, and somehow he found himself stumbling forward, seeing stars as the pommel of the leader's sword struck him on the back of his head.

Larian hit the deck hard, losing his breath for a second time.

He expected the killing blow to fall, but it never came. He heard scuffling above him, then a gurgling groan and a heavy thud next to him.

He turned his head and found himself looking into the brigand leader's wide, dead eyes. Forcing himself to his knees, he saw a knife buried hilt deep in the leader's solar plexus. Disbelieving, he looked up at Rosaline. She was breathing heavily, but appeared unharmed.

"How?"

She shrugged. "He lost focus, and I had another knife. Good

job distracting him, Larian." Rosaline took his hand and helped him to his feet. "Are you ok?"

"I will be in a minute." Rubbing the back of his head, he breathed deeply for several moments. Then a thought hit him. "You didn't see my armor anywhere did you? It's army issue, and I'll have to pay to replace it."

Rosaline nodded. "It's around the corner, with the rest of your stuff. That's where I found your sword."

"That's a relief."

They stepped around the corner and retrieved Larian's armor. It took several minutes to don it, even with Rosaline's help. Every time part of the armor clanked, Larian thought sure the remaining brigands must have heard, and would be coming running.

But that never happened. Although as he thought it through, Larian realized if they hadn't heard all the fighting, they wouldn't hear this comparatively soft noise. Still, where were they all?

"You look very handsome in your armor, Larian" Rosaline said as she tugged one of his chest straps tight.

"Wha-? Oh. Thanks. It feels good to wear, actually. Once it's all on, I almost don't feel the weight, it's balanced so well." He gave her a quick grin, then looked away, down the cave toward the next chamber.

"What are you looking for?"

"By my count, there should be six more of these guys here somewhere. They could come any minute."

"Oh." Rosaline stood, having finished tightening his straps, and looked away, biting her lip almost shyly.

"What's wrong?"

"Well...see, they kept me in a store room behind their sleeping quarters. After I did for my guard, I came out and found four of them asleep." She made a cutting gesture across her throat with her hand. "Then there was another one in the hall I managed to catch from behind. And I think I heard they were sending one guy to town for supplies."

Larian's jaw dropped. For a long moment, he was completely

speechless, then he started laughing uproariously. Rosaline frowned slightly and rested her hands on her hips.

"What's so funny?"

He raised his hand in a placating gesture. "It's just, well, I came here to rescue YOU, and it appears that was completely unnecessary."

Her frown changing into a gentle smile, Rosaline stepped forward and embraced him. "Larian, I love that you came to my rescue, but after they captured you..." He opened his mouth to speak, but she laid a finger on his lips, silencing him. "I've been saving myself for you. There's no way I was going to allow those...beasts...to have my maidenhood. Better to die fighting. You taught me that."

Larian blinked, then smiled sheepishly and gave her a long, lingering kiss. Eventually they parted, and he quipped "That's my girl. Let's get out of here."

It took the best part of the day to get back home. They arrived just after dusk, to the amazed delight of their neighbors, friends, and family.

That night, the town threw an impromptu party that turned into a full-on celebration when the citizens learned the brigands' fate. Later, after the party died down, Rosaline taught him another part of what it means to be a man.

The next day Larian's father awoke for the first time since the raid. The village healers were amazed, calling it a miracle.

Larian had three days before he had to depart to make it back in time before his leave expired. Those days passed quickly, but they were among the best he could recall in his entire life. All the same, when he left town, he reflected on his adventure and decided that when he got to his platoon, he was not going to speak a word of it to anyone.

Ever.

THE BLOB ON THE ROCK

"What am I looking at here?"

Margaret sounded annoyed, tired, confused, and determined all at once. She looked like hell, though Ray was not stupid enough to say so.

Instead, he activated the camera's zoom function. On the display in front of them, the image enlarged enough that there was no doubt.

"Son of a bitch," Margaret breathed, earning a nod of agreement from Ray.

"Never thought you'd see one of those, did you?" he replied, not bothering to suppress the satisfaction he felt.

Margaret had only grudgingly authorized this expedition, under the condition that she would supervise it personally. Ray had been halfway inclined to scrap the whole thing rather than endure that, but his partners forced his hand and he had reluctantly accepted the terms.

He could count on one hand the number of days, in the six months since, that he had not regretted that decision.

Margaret had made his life a living hell. Reports, projections, assessments, re-assessments of the assessments when results did not track with expectation, formal inquiries for every little thing that went wrong, the kind of inquiries that take a man-week or more to complete and leave you with nothing more than you started with at the beginning except piles of paperwork and several days of your life gone that you would never get back—all these and more she forced on him in the name of good management, procedural compliance, or whatever buzz phrase of the day she felt like latching on to.

It had gotten to the point that in a given day, he probably got two hours of real work done, max.

But today it was all worth it, because he was right.

Hot damn, he was right!

Even Margaret would not be able to deny it. Though she would try. Of that he had no doubt.

The door to the control room opened behind them and Ray turned to see Jusef, one of his partners, stroll in. Like everyone on the ship, he wore a loose light-grey jumpsuit that was belted at the waist and soft-soled shoes. This morning, he also wore a broad grin on his face.

Nodding in greeting, Jusef quipped, "What do you think of that, Maggie? Something, isn't it?"

Margaret scowled as she looked away from the display toward Jusef. She hated being called Maggie, something she had made abundantly clear over the years. But Jusef seemed to enjoy pushing her buttons. With no escape from each other in the ship's confines, Ray had thought Jusef would ease up.

No such luck.

"Yes, very interesting," Margaret replied in a clipped tone that generally meant she was about ready to chew some ass. "But hardly conclusive, in and of itself."

Ray felt his jaw drop. "What do you mean?" he said. "What else could..."

"I can think of half a dozen explanations off the top of my head, none of which conform to your hypothesis," she replied.

Jusef snorted and opened his mouth to retort, but stopped as Ray raised a calming hand.

"What would you suggest then?" Ray asked in as polite a tone as possible.

Margaret was silent for a moment as she looked back at the display and the image that grew slowly larger as their ship approached the object. Ray could not figure how there could be any doubt, but he was forced to admit it was more prudent to proceed from a skeptical point of view, however much he might not like it.

Finally, she spoke again.

"Continue gathering data and when we get close enough, collect a sample. If this," she gestured toward the slowly rotating object in the display, "is what you think it is, we should be able to tell easily enough once we get a close look at it."

Ray blinked in surprise. He glanced at Jusef, who wore a startled expression as well, one that faded into wariness quickly.

"Is that wise?" Jusef asked, his voice for once completely serious. "We don't know where it's from or what it can do. If we expose ourselves or contaminate the ship..."

Now it was time for Margaret to snort. "We have a clean room and bio-containment. Surely your team is competent to transport it without violating any of the protocols."

That went without saying. They were all exobiologists with extensive experience studying new organisms. Even Margaret, though by virtue or her position at the National Science Foundation she spent more time pushing paper and dealing with bureaucracy than anything else lately.

But this...

"This is different than anything we've ever encountered, Margaret," Ray said. "An organism that is born, lives, and dies, assuming it is does die, all in the vacuum of space. We can't know how it will react to a strong gravity well, let alone an atmosphere, severe heat..."

"Twenty-two degrees is hardly severe."

"It is when you live in negative two hundred sixty," Jusef pointed out.

Margaret flushed with what could only be embarrassment. That was a rookie mistake for a lay person, let alone a scientist. She had been out of the game for a while, Ray thought, but still.

"I don't think bringing it onboard is a good idea," Ray said, completing his earlier thought.

Margaret sniffed. Looking back at the display, she frowned slightly, then nodded. "Very well. Let's learn everything we can from afar. We may not need a sample at all." She looked back at Ray and whatever embarrassment she had felt a moment ago was gone, replaced by a steely expression of authority. "But I want the containment prepped and ready, just in case."

With that, she stalked out of the control room. As the door slid shut behind her, Jusef chuckled. "I thought this was your project, Ray."

"So did I," Ray replied with a rueful smile.

It was his idea. He was the one who ran the gauntlet of peer ridicule, funding pressure, and skepticism to get the expedition approved, however tight their budget ended up being.

Unfortunately, she who provides the money tends to make the rules in the real world.

"Well you heard her. Tell Charlie to get the containment facility ready."

Jusef nodded and took a step toward the door. It slid open and he paused, looking over his shoulder toward Ray. "Did you notice something?"

Ray shook his head. "No, what?"

"She gave over trying to deny what that thing is." Jusef grinned and waggled his eyebrows, then he stepped out of the room.

The door slid shut and Ray's smiled became broader, more genuinely happy. Jusef was right. How about that?

Ray watched with growing excitement as Eva, the ship's pilot and the only non-scientist aboard, keyed in the commands to bring the ship into a parallel orbit with the object they'd been approaching.

They were close now, only a kilometer away from it, and Ray could make out every detail with only minor use of the camera's zoom feature.

The asteroid was oblong, just over a hundred meters in length and a third of that wide, and tumbled end over end in a slow, awkward-looking rotation. It was nondescript, easily overlooked as just another hunk of mostly worthless elements floating through space.

Except for the darker lumps that speckled its surface.

Even they were nothing special to look at if one did so quickly. Only observing them for a moment or two revealed that they were moving across the asteroid's surface. And as each moved, it left behind a deep rift in the rock's surface.

The creatures, whatever they were, were eating the asteroid. Ray was sure of it.

"Alright Ray, we're parked," Eva said as she tapped shut one last dialogue window on her pilot's control station. Then she turned around and gave him a warm grin. "Have fun."

"You know it," he replied, and winked back.

She chuckled and shook her head in amusement, then leaned back in her chair to watch the fireworks, such as they were.

"Jusef," Ray began.

"Already on it. Spectrographic analyzer is online." At his work-station, Jusef leaned forward, peering intently at the readout from the analyzer. "Damn. The creatures' albedo is too low to get a good reading with this ambient light level. There's not enough light to work with. I'll have to flash them." He frowned and chewed on his lip for a moment, then looked over at Ray.

Ray thought about it for a minute.

The creatures might be sensitive to light; living in space the way they did, it was only logical they would get at least some of their energy from nearby stars. He did not want to disturb or harm them. On the other hand, the analyzer's flash was brief and in a discreet frequency band, so the chance of causing undue stress was rather low.

And they needed information.

He nodded. "Ok, go ahead."

Jusef returned the nod and said, "Here goes nothing."

He tapped a command into his workstation. A moment later, powerful lights mounted beneath the ship's hull illuminated a targeted area of the asteroid briefly. Jusef's display lit up as data streamed across it.

His eyes widened.

"Arsenic-based from the looks of it. A few complex compounds...this one looks almost like chlorophyl, but not quite." He leaned back and looked over at Ray. "It'll take a while to fully analyze, but this thing is a beauty!"

"Outstanding," Ray said, grinning. He loved being right. He really did. Glancing over at Margaret, sitting at her observation workstation in the corner, he was gratified to see her eyes wide in amazement. "Charlie?"

Off to his left, Charlie cleared his throat and replied, "Looks like they average a meter and a half long by three quarters of a meter wide. Radar mapping has them moving at an average of ten centimeters per minute and leaving a trail an average of six centimeters deep in their path. Infrared puts them at 5 degrees above background."

"Warm blooded?" Margaret said a bit breathlessly. "How is that possible in this environment?"

"That's what we're here to find out, Margaret," Ray said, hardly able to contain his excitement. He couldn't help himself. He looked back at her, winked, and quipped, "Oh ye of little faith."

She glowered at him for a moment, then smirked and nodded. "True enough. Though I don't see how you'll be able to figure that out without examining a specimen up close."

Ray sighed. "You're probably right." Looking back at the display, he tapped his fingers on the top of his workstation desk.

Charlie piped up, "If we grab one, we'll need to take a piece of the asteroid as well. It'll be easier to just scoop it out than to try to remove the thing from the rock. I can set up the containment to simulate the exterior conditions as closely as possible. Then all we have to do is configure the sample container to maintain micro-gravity during transport in and out of containment." He smiled slightly. "Not too hard."

Ray thought about it for a minute. Despite his and Jusef's earlier resistance to Margaret's notion, he had, in the back of his mind, considered the possibility of doing an EVA to retrieve a sample of whatever they found. It was not anything he hadn't done before, really.

Still...

"What do you think, Jusef?"

Jusef frowned and leaned forward, peering at the main display through narrowed eyes. "I don't know. There's a lot that can go wrong."

"Oh please." Margaret sounded annoyed again. As usual. "Can you really tell me you'll be able to learn much more of use from way out here?" There was a brief period of silence, then she nodded to herself. "I didn't think so."

Ray and Jusef traded glances. Jusef rolled his eyes, no doubt thinking the same thing Ray was.

If only she would leave them alone to do their work, things would be so much easier.

Ray sighed. "Alright, Margaret. We'll do it your way. Charlie, prep for an EVA."

The creature resting on the hunk of rock in the middle of the containment area did not look like anything special. Just a green-brown blob atop a grey-brown surface.

It was the coolest thing Ray had ever seen.

As promised, Charlie had adjusted the containment area to

match conditions outside the ship as closely as they were able. The creature should be relatively comfortable.

"Ok. Now what?"

It was almost like Jusef was reading Ray's mind. Ray shrugged. "No idea. Charlie?"

"We could try adjusting conditions, applying some stimulation. See how it responds."

Ray frowned as he considered Charlie's words. "What did you have in mind? I don't want to hurt it."

"Raise the ambient light level a bit?"

"I guess that can't do any harm. Go ahead."

Charlie nodded and turned to the containment area's control workstation.

Through the one-way viewing window, Ray could see the light levels increase perceptibly. They waited for several minutes, but nothing happened.

He nodded in response to a questioning look from Charlie, then waited as the other man raised the light level again.

Still nothing. Charlie raised the light level a third time.

The creature seemed to shrink in on itself and darken. That could not be good.

"Turn it down," Ray commanded, and within seconds Charlie had the lights back down to their original setting.

The creature slowly returned to its original size and, from what Ray could tell in the lower lighting, its original color. He breathed a sigh of relief that was echoed by the others with him.

"That was interesting," Jusef remarked.

The intercom beeped and Eva's face appeared on the display. She looked a bit worried.

"Ray, I just detected a burst of radio waves."

He could feel his eyebrows raising on his forehead. "Radio? From where?"

"Hard to say. The directional is not giving me a good reading. It's almost as if..." She frowned. "I'd say it came from us, but we haven't been transmitting." Something offscreen caught her attention and her frown deepened. "Another burst of radio. The directional got a read this time. It's..." Her eyes widened. "It's coming from the asteroid."

"What?"

Behind him, Margaret interjected, "Maybe we're not the first ones here."

Ray shook his head. "Not a chance. Did you hear of any other projects like ours?"

Silence was her answer. Ray looked around to see her biting her lip nervously. Finally, she shook her head. "What's causing it then?"

No one said anything for a long time Ray had a suspicion, but it was so unlikely...

He caught himself in mid-thought and gave himself a mental shake. Very little in nature was actually impossible. What if...

He looked back at the creature in the containment area and felt another surge of excitement.

"Eva, stand by," he said. "Charlie, raise the light level again, please. Slowly."

Charlie nodded, an eager light in his eyes. He suspected the same thing Ray did, apparently.

"What are you doing?" Margaret asked.

She moved forward from her observer's station to stand next to Ray, between him and Jusef. He glanced to the side, annoyance welling up for a moment. It was crowded enough without having someone pushing people around.

But then he saw her expression. Nervousness had given way to actual fear.

She *had* been out of the game for a while. He reminded himself that looking a new life form in the eye in the depths of space is far different from making policy decisions in an office in Washington, DC.

"Just watch," Ray said with a smile he hoped was reassuring. "This should be interesting."

The light level in the containment area gradually increased in response to Charlie's command. As before, nothing happened for a time.

Then, suddenly, the creature again shrank and darkened.

Charlie looked at Ray. "Turn it down?"

"Just a moment." Ray glanced at the intercom display. "Eva?"

Her reply was instant. "More radio transmissions, no good direction. What are you doing down there?"

"Confirming a hypothesis. Keep monitoring." With that, he turned back to Charlie and gestured for him to lower the lights again.

Very quickly, the ambient light in the containment area was back to its original setting. The creature reacted as it had before, returning to its original configuration.

"Any change, Eva?"

She nodded. "Radio transmissions have stopped."

"I'd say that confirms it," Jusef said with a grin. "They communicate with each other using radio waves."

"Astounding," Margaret breathed. Her nervousness was obviously fading. She leaned toward the viewing window to get a better look. "I've never heard of such a thing."

"It's not that unbelievable," Charlie replied. "Eels on earth can generate an electric current. It's not far from that to generating a radio signal."

"Yes, but to encode it, to make it coherent..."

Jusef snorted. "Let's not get ahead of ourselves. It's not like they're transmitting television or something."

Before Ray could interject, Eva gasped in surprise and shock over the intercom. He blinked; she was normally a very cool customer.

"Eva, what's up?"

"More transmissions from the asteroid," she replied. "The amplitude is more intense and the duration longer. I'm not sure what..." She looked at a display offscreen then cursed and went pale. When her gaze returned to the intercom, there was noticeable tension in her face and shoulders. "We've got a problem, Ray."

Eva tapped a command and her face was replaced with a view of the asteroid. It still tumbled slowly through space, carrying its unusual cargo. But Ray immediately saw what had caused Eva's chagrin.

Two green-brown blobs, larger than the others by several meters from the look of them, had detached themselves from the asteroid and were moving toward the ship.

"Aw hell," Charlie said. "It's Mom and Dad."

Back in the control room, Ray peered at the contact evaluation plot on the main display screen.

The two creatures were depicted as red Xs with velocity vectors displaying their speeds and projected closest points of approach to the ship. By most standards, they were not moving very quickly, just 5 meters per second. But they were on an intercept course with the ship and would arrive in less than three minutes.

"Now this is interesting," Ray said, looking from the plot to the camera display.

Detached from the asteroid, the creatures' undersides were visible. They had multitudes of flexible limbs that were capped by what appeared to be suction cups, but no mouth or eyes. Ears were out of the question, of course; they would be useless in the void. But where were the rest of the creatures' organs and tools?

They would be a fascinating study in a proper laboratory.

"I guess that's one way to describe it," Eva said. "What are we going to do? I doubt they're coming over for a friendly chat."

Charlie nodded concurrence. "If this is a display of parental protectiveness..."

"Or just a herd mentality," Jusef interjected.

Charlie sighed and nodded, conceding the point. "Either way, they're likely to be violent."

A loud snort was Margaret's initial reply. "They're floating blobs with suckers. How violent can they be?"

Ray tapped the command console and zoomed in on the asteroid, specifically on the grooves each of the creatures left in the rock. "Look at that, Margaret. I'm not sure we want to see what they can do to our ship's hull."

They sat in silence for a few seconds, considering. Glancing around, Ray saw frowns on every face.

There were no good decisions. They could just maneuver away; they could easily outrun the creatures at their current pace. But then they would lose the opportunity to study them in greater detail. They could release the creature down in containment and hope that, with its return, the others would calm down and go back to what they were doing. Or they could try to repel the approaching creatures.

Although exactly how they would accomplish that was another good question. Science vessels do not carry weapons, by and large, and this ship was no exception.

"I don't want to lose the opportunity to study them," Jusef said and received murmurs of concurrence from everyone in the room.

"Alright then. Jusef, try hitting them with the lights again, full spectrum this time." Jusef nodded but paused as Ray continued. "Charlie, go down to containment and get ready to bring the creature back outside." He noticed all eyes on him, none of them pleased, and he added. "Just in case."

Margaret scowled darkly but remained silent as Charlie got up and hurried out of the room.

It took a few keystrokes to reconfigure the strobes. By the time Jusef was ready, the creatures were two-thirds of the way to the ship. The tension in the control room was palpable by the time Jusef nodded in readiness.

"Ok, hit them."

At Ray's command, Jusef activated the strobes. There was an immediate reaction from the oncoming creatures.

They darkened, and the receiver indications at Eva's console lit up like a christmas tree as they transmitted their radio signal.

But they kept on coming. In fact, they increased speed.

Ray swallowed, a chill going up his spine as he looked at the plot and saw their speed had doubled. No wait, tripled. He keyed the intercom. "Charlie, are you ready?"

Charlie shook his head and Ray could see he was halfway into donning a spacesuit. "It's gonna be a couple minutes."

"We don't have a couple minutes. Hurry up."

Ray turned to Eva, who looked at the plot as though poleaxed. "Eva, move us away." She did not move, so he shouted more loudly, "Eva!"

Eva shook herself and acknowledged, then tapped in the sequence of commands that activated the ship's thrusters.

Ray felt a few seconds' acceleration, then in the main camera display, the asteroid began growing smaller. On the plot, the creatures' rate of closure reduced quickly and then went to zero.

"That will give us some time to think," Ray said, trying to sound more calm than he felt. "Jusef, turn the lights off."

"Already done." Jusef looked as though he really was calm. He tapped his index finger on his lips in thought as he watched the creatures on the display. "Very interesting. It's almost as though light hurts them, but also gives them energy."

"Yeah." Jusef was right. It was interesting. But it was not the top priority at the moment. "I'm going to tell Charlie to release it from containment. Any objections?"

Eva shook her head quickly. Amazingly enough, Margaret was right behind her. Jusef looked for a moment as though he was going to raise an objection, but instead shook his head, frowning.

"Alright." Ray keyed the intercom again. "Charlie, as soon as you're ready, release it."

On the camera display, the small creature drifted away from the ship on its small asteroid fragment.

For a minute or so nothing happened. Then, all of a sudden, it detached from the hunk of rock. Several of the suction cups on the ends of its limbs made a burping motion and it began moving toward the two larger creatures.

They, in turn, altered their course toward it.

Ray let out a breath that he hadn't realized he'd been holding. "Looks like they're going for it," he murmured.

The creatures met and the smaller one made a tight circle around the other two, trailing its limbs over their backs in a strangely intimate display. After that, first one then the other larger creatures made a similar circle around the small one. The trio went on like that for several minutes, trading off circling caresses in sequence.

Then they stopped, clustered together in a tight formation.

"I guess that takes care of that... Aw hell."

Charlie could have been speaking for all of them. On the display, the small creature and one of the large pair split off and sped away back toward the asteroid, now just a small point of light in the distance. They moved far faster than before.

But the other large creature remained still for a long moment, then rotated in space and shot toward the ship, again at a much faster clip than it had used earlier.

"Crap," Eva shouted, and she punched the thruster controls.

They were pressed into their seats as the ship accelerated away, but the creature was was already going too fast. Inexorably, it grew larger in the display screen.

"Impact in thirty seconds," Eva reported, her voice strained but even.

"Any ideas?" Ray asked, and received silence in response.

Eva tapped another command and the ship lurched to the side, nearly throwing them out of their seats.

On the display, the creature zipped past, but quickly adjusted to their new vector as it continued to close the distance between them.

It was no use. They were going to collide.

"Brace for impact!," Eva shouted.

The creature filled the entire camera display, then the ship rang like a gong. They *were* thrown out of their chairs this time as the ship turned completely over. It took a long several seconds for the inertial systems to compensate and restore the gravity vector to normal, and they bounced around erratically the whole time.

When they finally came to rest, Ray came down hard on his left shoulder. Pain flared up from the joint and his arm went numb; a bad sign. Gritting his teeth to fight against the pain, he forced himself to his feet.

"Everyone ok?"

Assorted grunts and groans were the only answer. But one by one, the other three got to their feet. They looked alright. That was something, at least.

"Eva, status report please?"

Just then a loud hissing and popping sound echoed through the ship, followed by a deep groaning.

"What's that?" Margaret asked, her face ashen and her voice strained.

"My guess is the creature is trying to eat the ship, the same way it eats that asteroid," Jusef replied.

"Is there anything we can do?"

Great question. Ray looked over at Eva, who shook her head. "Short of doing an EVA and manually prying it off the hull, no."

"How long would that take?"

She snorted. "How do you intend to do it is the better question."

There was a long silence after that. Ray did a mental tally of their onboard equipment and was forced to concede her point. They did not have anything that could even begin to dislodge something as large as that creature.

"So we're screwed," Charlie summed up, apparently having done the same calculation in his head.

"Looks that way," Ray said. "Ok. Charlie, get all the data we've collected collated and transmit it to the Kranz Station. Eva, get the lifeboat powered up. The rest of you gather up your gear and all the food and water you can carry. There's no telling how long a rescue will take."

He rose and moved toward the door, but Margaret stepped in his way.

"This is insane. You can't know that it will be able to get through the hull."

"It's just a matter of time, if it keeps working at it."

"And what's to stop it from coming after us in the lifeboat?"

Ray sighed, feeling the others' eyes on him as he replied. "Nothing. Our best hope is that it's so focused on taking the ship out that it won't notice us when we launch."

"And if it isn't?"

He shrugged and her face dropped. He thought he saw the beginning of tears in her eyes for a moment. Then, with a swift inhalation, she wiped her eyes and nodded. "We'd better get to it, then."

Right then, in spite of himself, Ray found he admired her.

Through the lifeboat's viewing window, Ray watched as their ship died.

First one, then a second stream of gasses began venting from the vessel as the creature chewed through the hull and into the innards of the ship. The ship began rotating erratically under the force of the venting gasses and then, suddenly, blew apart in a quickly extinguished flash of flame.

The creature must have contacted the fuel lines.

Ray almost hoped the creature had been killed in the blast, but his intellect rebelled against such gross barbarity. It wasn't the creature's fault that they had come barging in to its home and carried off its child.

Jusef had earlier been quick to point out that there was no evidence the creatures were displaying family instincts, but Ray found he preferred to think they did.

It made them less alien and inscrutable, more human almost.

In the expanding ring of wreckage, Ray saw the creature right itself and rotate around in space for a moment. His breath caught in his throat.

This was it. Would it come after them again?

The seconds ticked by, each one seeming to take hours. Then, slowly, the creature began moving. Back toward the asteroid.

Ray breathed a sigh of relief and heard the same from his shipmates.

Smiling for the first time in what felt like years, he turned away from the viewing window. On the other side of the lifeboat, Eva had a set of earphones pressed to her ear. She nodded excitedly and said, "Roger, out."

Her smile as she turned to face the rest of them was like sunlight on a cloudy day. "They say the rescue will be here by this time tomorrow," she reported.

Combined with his relief over the creature's departure, the news made Ray feel like dancing a jig. Alas, there was not enough room for that. So he did the next best thing he could think of. Sitting down in one of the chairs that surrounded the table in the middle of the room, he looked his companions in the eyes one at a time and grinned.

"Anyone up for a game of cards?"

FALLING SOFTLY

Through his spyglass, the assassin watched Lord Padmar disembark his carriage. He was dressed in his best: a dark red coat with gold buttons, loose about the shoulders and tight at the forearms and belly, an off-white ruffled shirt with lace at the throat and cuffs, tight black leggings that tucked into polished, knee-high, black turned-down boots, and a golden sash from right shoulder to left hip. He wore a jaunty hat of the same color as his coat and a broad black leather belt that supported a gold-pommeled saber on his right hip. The rumors said he actually knew how to use it, a rarity among the upper nobility these days.

The Lord strode quickly to the front door of his manor, where his chamberlain waited. In his late middle years, the chamberlain was tall, but portly, with thinning gray hair. He stood with a pronounced slouch, probably from a lifetime spent bowing and scraping. The Lord spoke with him briefly before he went inside, not bothering to acknowledge the other servants' deep bows.

The chamberlain lingered for a moment. He looked around, his back to the other servants, then nodded and touched his right thumb to the tip of his middle finger and raised both to the center of his chest. That was the signal: all was in readiness.

The assassin smiled thinly. Lord Padmar was well known as an overbearing, sanctimonious, and cruel employer. Among the serving class, tales of the punishments he doled out for the smallest infractions were legendary, leaving only the most desperate willing to even entertain the notion of going into his service. The chamberlain was immune from the worst of those punishments, but all the same it was ridiculously easy, and cheap, for the assassin's representative to obtain his cooperation in this night's hit.

Lord Padmar, it turned out, was a man of habit. The assassin had been watching him for three weeks, and knew his routine by heart. Tonight was his weekly card game at Viscount Ephrim's estate. The Lord always returned promptly at four bells, and was in bed by five. Padmar's wife found her own entertainment on this night each week: she had a lover in a manor outside the city. It strained credulity to think Padmar didn't know, but clearly he didn't care. Most weeks, a high-priced companion was ushered in through a side door before he arrived and awaited him in his bedchamber. Perfect.

Putting down the spyglass, the assassin slithered back from the roof edge. Careful to avoided showing a silhouette, he rolled behind one of the many chimneys atop the building. Vargas was there, waiting. Clad the same as the assassin, in loose-fitting black clothing that covered him from head to toe save his eyes, he carried a longbow and a full quiver. A long-bladed knife was sheathed on his left thigh.

"All set?"

The assassin nodded quickly. "I'm going in. Keep a sharp eye out."

"I always do."

With that, Vargas slipped around the chimney, flattening himself along its side. From the distance, it would be impossible to pick him out from the chimney itself. The assassin slid backwards to the other side of the roof. At the edge of the building, there was a drainpipe that served to keep the flat roof clear of rainwater. It was perfect for climbing, and in less than a minute, he had descended the forty feet to the street.

He moved swiftly along the building's wall, keeping to the shadows. He paused when he reached the corner and pulled a small mirror from a pouch on his belt then extended it past the edge. The coast was clear.

Slipping around the corner, he dropped to the ground and slithered beneath a series of open windows, only standing again when he reached the next edge of the building. Directly across the street was the fence marking the boundary of the Lord's estate. Ten feet high, made of wrought iron and topped with spear-like spikes, it wouldn't be much of a challenge.

He checked the street with his mirror, then pressed back as he spied a carriage moving toward him. Hardly breathing, he remained absolutely still. The Lamplighter's Guild had already made their rounds, and though he had broken the lamps on either side of this intersection earlier in the day, there was still more light than he would have preferred.

The carriage, a plain but well crafted model with room enough for four in back, passed slowly. The driver never looked away from the road, but the curtains in the passenger compartment were open. If any of the passengers saw him, it would mean trouble. But the carriage never stopped, and after a few minutes it turned a corner and vanished from sight.

The assassin checked the street again. If he was going to be undone, it would be in the crossing. No one in sight, it was now or never.

He took a deep breath and sprinted across to the fence. A quick leap and he had ahold of two of the spikes. Pulling his feet up to the crossbar at the top of the fence, he hung there for a few moments. Then he heaved himself upward and over the fence. Tucking into a roll as he hit the ground, he came to his feet smoothly and waited, motionless.

The Lord had guards who patrolled the fence line regularly. If the chamberlain had done his part, they would be late turning over the watch, and the assassin would have a window of a few minutes. But he hadn't survived as long as he had in this business by assuming things would go smoothly. He listened carefully for a while, but there was nothing but the normal sounds of night creatures. Satisfied he was safe, he moved out.

The manor house was about a hundred yards ahead, beyond a stand of trees and a manicured garden. He made the distance quickly, darting from cover to cover to avoid being seen.

He approached the house from the side, where a large patio area was partially covered by a good-sized balcony extending out from the second story of the house. That balcony should lead to the Lord's chambers. The columns holding the balcony up were round, about a foot in diameter, and smooth. He managed to shimmy up the one at the corner without too much trouble.

As he peeked over the balcony railing, the assassin was gratified to see the double doors leading into the house, a well-crafted pair with large inset windows, were ajar. The chamberlain had come through again.

There were a couple of cushioned chairs on the balcony and a small table. The assassin was careful not to disturb them as he boosted himself over the railing. It wouldn't do to make any noise now. Creeping across to the door, he could see curtains drawn on the other side, blocking his view of the chambers within.

The assassin crouched in the doorway and slowly opened the door on his right the rest of the way. Good thing it opened outward. Slowly pushing the curtain aside, he peered inside the room. His eyes, already well adjusted to the moonless night, picked out the details without too much difficulty. A large, four posted bed hung with mosquito netting sat against the far wall. A small round table with two chairs was off to the left and a large armoire rested against the wall on the assassin's right. Two closed doors were visible on either side of the bed.

As he moved into the room, the assassin's soft-soled shoes barely made a whisper. He could make out two lumps in the bed and heard soft snoring from the left side. He approached the right side first.

The woman was barely covered by the sheets. Even in the near blackness, the assassin could tell that she was stunning: well curved hips, full breasts. Too bad what was going to happen to her.

He reached into another belt pouch and withdrew a small vial. Parting the mosquito netting, he unstoppered the vial and slowly, carefully, poured several drops of its contents into the woman's open mouth.

She stirred slightly, and he froze. But she just turned her head and settled down again after a moment. He was gratified to see her swallow. The potion should keep her asleep for several hours.

The assassin moved around the bed to the Lord's side, re-stoppering the bottle and replacing it in his pouch as he went. As he parted the netting, he drew a long, narrow-bladed dagger from a sheath on his thigh.

The assassin placed his hand over the Lord's mouth, and his eyes opened wide. The assassin gave him no time to struggle, though, stabbing him in the chest, neck, and belly.

The Lord tried to scream at first, but the hand over his mouth allowed only a muffled groan that quickly became a series of gurgling coughs. He grasped at his wounds, but they were too many and any one of them would have been fatal. It was over in under a minute, and the assassin removed his hand.

He took a moment to clean up, pulling a rag from a pocket on his hip and wiping the blood from his gloves and clothing. It wouldn't do at all to leave a blood trail when he departed.

When he was done, he put the rag back into his pocket and moved back to the woman's side of the bed. His last act before heading back out to the balcony was to place the knife in her hand and give her a gentle kiss on her forehead.

The assassin was out of the room and across the manor grounds in less than two minutes. He took a course toward the fence a short distance from where he made his initial crossing, pulling his mirror from its pouch as he drew near.

There was a large tree growing right up near the fence and a street lamp on the other side. Crouching against the tree, he angled the mirror to reflect the lamp light toward the chimney where Vargas was stationed. A moment later, he saw a brief flash from next to the chimney. Vargas had struck flint and steel: one spark for all's clear.

The assassin sped back to his initial crossing point and vaulted the fence in the same manner as before, then raced across the street. He met Vargas behind the building just as the other man was finishing his descent of the drain pipe.

"Any issues?" inquired Vargas.

"None. Let's go get paid."

The pair ducked down a side street, still keeping to the shadows, and cut a zig-zag course through the city. If they had missed someone seeing them, it wouldn't do to offer a direct route to follow.

Behind his mask, the assassin smiled. This was their highest profile target yet, and the down payment alone was enough to live well for a year or more. The final payment promised to leave them in luxury for quite some time. Taken with what he'd saved from their other jobs, it might just be enough to get out of the business altogether. He wasn't made of stone, after all. Sooner or later, he wanted to lead a normal life, start a family, that sort of thing. But on his own terms, and certainly not in poverty.

The assassin and Vargas reached the designated spot at seven bells. At the edge of the port district, the warehouse was smaller than most, and saw only limited use. Real Estate was too valuable in the city to just leave a building empty, but the rising trading power of Meribor, 200 miles or so to the south, had attracted a number of ships that used to port here. So sometimes the building was half full, sometimes it was nearly empty. That led the building's owner to let it out, on occasion, for less than legal dealings.

The pair split up as they approached: the assassin headed for the back door while Vargas scaled the side of the building itself, again using a drain pipe. There was a stairwell from the rooftop to the upper level scaffolding inside the warehouse, and Vargas would take position there with his bow, in case anything went wrong.

Vargas almost never met directly with clients. He had no mind for negotiation and besides, just as when he was doing the job, the assassin needed Vargas to watch his back. There was no less danger here than in the Lord's manor. In fact, in some ways there was actually more.

The back door was unlocked, and the assassin slipped inside without a sound.

Inside, the warehouse was mostly open except for some offices in the front. It was about one quarter filled with boxes of various sizes. For this evening's event, there was a table set up in the middle of the warehouse. The area was lit by a number of lamps, but all the windows were covered with heavy cloth, to prevent the light from escaping into the street. The assassin could see his employer sitting at the table, dressed as before in dark grey cowled robes and a black mask of a frowning face. Two guards stood behind him, a small chest between them. No one else was visible. Everything looked in order.

The assassin walked up to the table. Stopping two paces away, he watched the three men warily. His employer spoke first.

"It is done?"

The assassin nodded. "Just as you asked. In the morning, the servants and guards will find the Lord dead and put the blame on the woman. No one will believe the word of a whore, no matter how high priced." He shrugged his shoulders, adding "Too bad, it looked like she was good."

"Excellent. Your reward is well earned. Gomly, pay him."

The guard to the employer's right nodded and fished a key out of his pocket. As he bent over to unlock the chest, he blocked the assassin's view of the second guard for a fatal moment.

Gomly stood, a jingling sack in his hand, and the second guard reached behind this back, pulled out a small crossbow, pointed it at the assassin and pulled the trigger.

Although he knew trouble was possible, the assassin had begun to relax when Gomly went to the chest. Thus, he was surprised at the attack. Still, his reflexes were good, and he leapt to the side as soon as the crossbow pointed his way.

He was not fast enough, though. The assassin felt a crushing impact in his lower left abdomen, and he was knocked to the floor. Searing pain, beyond anything he had ever felt, filled his brain. He clutched at the wound, only to find that the quarrel had gone so far in that its head protruded out the small of his back.

Vargas! Help! He wanted to shout the words, but nothing came out but a loud groan of pain.

The whistling sound of an arrow's flight, followed by a squishy THUNK, then a scream and a thud indicated that Vargas had entered the fray. The assassin rolled over and saw his employer crouched behind the table, the guard with the crossbow down with an arrow in his chest.

He managed to feel a bit of hope. Vargas had saved his ass more than once, after all. Then he heard a shout of surprise followed by a horrified scream from above. He turned his head just in time to see Vargas land headfirst on the floor after a fall from the scaffolding, about twenty-five feet above.

Biting back another scream, this one of despair, the assassin turned his attention back to his (former) employer. He had regained his feet and was walking slowly toward him.

No. It couldn't end like this. He tried to get away, but all he could manage was a slow, agonized crawl.

"It's no use, my friend. I have men at every door" said his employer as he approached.

The assassin could see it was true, but he had to keep trying. All the same, he felt his limbs weakening, and he began to grow dizzy from blood loss. Gasping for breath, he managed to crawl another five feet or so before his employer reached him. Gomly placed his foot beneath the assassin's shoulder and kicked him onto his back. Another stab of pain flared through his side as the quarrel shifted in his wound.

Looking up at Gomly and his employer, all the tales the assassin had heard from his parents and various clergymen about Deus, and the judgment of souls in the afterlife, came rushing to the front of his mind. He'd always scoffed at such things, but now, facing his end, he felt an all-consuming dread. What if it were all true?

"Please..." gasped the assassin. "Please. I need a priest."

His employer, standing over him with his arms crossed, shook his head slowly. "Won't do you any good, I'm afraid. Absolution requires confession *and* repentance. And you, my friend, have no time to prove your repentance with deeds."

He stepped back and gestured for Gomly to proceed.

The guard nodded and drew his sword. The assassin watched with helpless horror as Gomly plunged the blade into his chest.

He didn't feel it, a small mercy. The world began to fade around him, and he felt a deep regret that he had never really lived. Then darkness engulfed him, and his regret turned to terror as he perceived the first flickering of the flames awaiting him on the other side.

THE MEMORY OF JUSTICE

The world was a blur of shadows and splotches of color that swirled around as Jacob turned his head from side to side. After a while, its lack of cohesion just added to the ache in his temples, turning a dull throb into stabbing pain that made him grit his teeth to hold back a groan.

At least he had teeth; a strangely comforting bit of normalcy, that.

Jacob tried to rub his brow but found his hands were restrained. He could not move them from his sides. After a moment's concentration, he realized they were resting on thin pieces of a grainy material - wood? Pressure on his back and bottom came into focus then, and he realized he was sitting in a chair, with his hands on its arms.

He blinked, and the world stopped swirling so much, coming to resemble merely an amorphous blob. An improvement. Looking down, he could just barely make out the shapes of his arms and legs, and that of the chair. But he still could not move; his arms and legs must have been bound to the chair.

Where was he? How had he gotten here?

He had no idea, and no memory of anything after Clara...

The name went through his mind like a jolt of electricity.

Sudden fear swept through him, masking his earlier anxiety beneath its weight. Was she a prisoner too?

Jacob tried to call out to her, but all that came from his mouth was a rough grunt. His mouth was dry as a desert at midday, making it difficult to sound out words, and there was an awful metallic taste lingering on his palette.

He closed his mouth and worked his jaw but saliva would not come, despite the hunger pangs that he was only just beginning to recognize for what they were. How long had he been here?

The world changed.

Light, brighter than anything else had been, stabbed into his eyes, and he recoiled. As much as he was able to recoil, restrained as he was. He blinked several times in rapid succession, willing the new purple spots to clear from his vision so he could tell what was going on.

Slowly, the glare reduced, or rather his eyes adjusted to it. And as they did so, his surroundings became more clear.

The room was not large, but roomy. The walls were off-white, probably the default paint job the original builders had applied. His chair was near the center of the floor, which was hardwood but covered in a cheap rug where he sat. Mostly-empty bookshelves lined the wall to his left; to his right was a closed hardwood door that was painted blue. There were no windows. The wall in front of him was dominated by a large video display and its control terminal. The display was dark, but a small, lit LED on its lower right corner indicated its readiness.

The light that had dazzled him so came from two large directional lamps, one in either corner of the room ahead of him. Both were turned to shine directly at him. It reminded him of the interrogation rooms cliché bad guys use in bad thriller movies.

It even smelled like he imagined such places would: clean, antiseptic, with just a hint of a cleaning solution lingering in the air.

The fear did not go away; it intensified. What the hell was going on?

A soft click drew his gaze to the right, to the door.

The knob was beginning to turn. Someone was coming in.

Jacob tried to steel himself, prepare for what was to come. It was not going to be pleasant; he knew that in his gut.

Then the door opened, and his fear gave way to surprised shock as a lean woman of medium height strode into the room. She wore jeans and a loose-fitting burgundy shirt that buttoned up the front, and athletic shoes. Her hair, red-brown and pulled back into a pony tail, framed an oval face that was dominated by a slightly-too-large nose.

His shock at seeing her here, like this, almost caused him to miss the fact that she carried a semi-automatic pistol in her right hand.

"Hello Jacob," Clara said. "We have some things to discuss."

Jacob shut the tap and turned back to the bar, foamy mug in hand. Lawrence waited on his usual stool, with the same expectant expression on his face as he always did. When Jacob slid the mug across to him, he grinned - again, the same lopsided grin as always - and waved his hand over the payment processing sensor. Jacob did not need to look to see how much of a tip Lawrence had left; that was always the same as well. Hell, if the man did not occasionally change ties, Jacob would be unable to tell whether he had ever left the bar.

Jacob found it quite boring; he wondered if Lawrence did as well.

"Heard about that guy they have on trial?"

Jacob shrugged. He did not pay attention to that kind of news. Too depressing. Besides, Lawrence was just going to tell him about it anyway.

To pass the time, Jacob fished a rag out of the sink next to the taps and began wiping the bar down. The darkly stained wood got dusty or stained from spilled drinks or glasses without coasters if he did not wipe it down a couple times a shift, and the owner hated that.

Not that there was much concern of spilled drinks tonight; it was Tuesday, and the place was empty except for Lawrence.

"Legal expert on the News thinks sure the jury's gonna decide guilty." Lawrence swallowed a gulp of his beer and burped softly before continuing. "Says the DA is pushing for a total memory wipe."

"That right."

Lawrence nodded, his head resembling a bobble-head doll for a moment. This was his last drink for the night. He would bitch about it, but the last thing Jacob needed was to clean up more barf.

"Not sure what I think of that." Lawrence looked down into his mug for a long moment. "It'd almost be more humane just to shoot him, you know?"

Right. Gun him down like a rabid dog. Real humane.

"Lawrence, I think you've had..."

The door swung open, drawing his gaze away from a stain that had somehow escaped his earlier wiping. When he saw the woman entering, he lost track of what she was about to say.

She glanced over at Lawrence, but quickly dismissed him, instead focusing on Jacob. Her eyes, green he thought, flickered up and down, taking him in, or as much of him as was visible above the bar anyway, and her lips turned upward into a small smile that made her face light up.

"You still serving dinner?"

"The kitchen just closed," Jacob said. Her smile faded as quickly as it appeared. He added, "But I think I can rustle something up."

She sidled up to a stool at the far end of the bar from Lawrence. "Thanks. I'm starving, and I need a beer."

"That's what I'm here for. I'm Jacob."

The woman took his hand in a gentle, but strong, grip and smiled more broadly. "Clara. Clara Cumberland."

"Clara, what...?"

She made a soft tsking noise. Moving with the languid grace he had admired from the first time he met her, six weeks before when she first walked into the bar, she stepped in front of his chair and leaned forward until her face was at eye level with him.

Those deep green eyes, which always before had flashed with humor and warmth, were cold, sharp.

"Shh, pigeon," she said, and he felt something cold and hard touch his left cheek. "Things will become," the hard metal of the pistol's front sight traced a line down his cheek, then across his chin as she spoke, "very clear soon enough." She smiled then, a mirthless grin that only enhanced the ice in her gaze, and stepped back from him.

He imagined he could still feel the touch of the gun against his skin as she crossed her arms and turned away, toward the display control station. What was she playing at?

"You do not remember when we first met." She spoke without turning around, instead tapping the control station to bring it to life.

"Sure I do. You had just finished unpacking and came in for dinner and a beer because you didn't feel like..."

"*No!*"

Clara rounded on him, her eyes flashing angrily for a second before she schooled her face to calm ice one more. She took a deep breath, then spoke again, more calmly.

"We did not meet six weeks ago, pigeon. You don't remember our first meeting, but I will never forget." She lowered her gaze and took another deep breath, and it was obvious Clara was forcing down some deep emotions.

What was she talking about? Jacob had never seen her before that night in the bar, he was sure of it. He opened his mouth to retort, but found the words frozen in his mouth as Clara looked back up, her frosty eyes meeting his in a gaze he could not look away from, and spoke again.

"Five years ago today, you raped and murdered my sister."

Stunned, Jacob just stared at Clara for what seemed an hour but in fact was probably more like thirty seconds. He had done *what*? How could she think him capable of such a thing? In his entire life, he had never laid hands on a woman, even those who really needed to be slapped or otherwise stopped from hurting themselves or others, namely him.

When he was little - three, maybe four - Jacob got into a fight with his sister, God rest her soul, and kicked her. His father had taken his belt to Jacob's bottom, then explained the reality of life in no uncertain terms. A boy - a man - does not strike, or in any way harm, a girl. Ever. For any reason.

No matter what.

"Clara, you have me confused with someone else. I've never..."

Instead of replying, Clara tapped the remote control - he had not noticed that she picked it up - and the wall display lit up.

A news broadcast began to play. It was five years old from the time stamp on the lower left corner of the screen. It showed a body being rolled into an ambulance. The entire scene was blocked off by yellow crime scene tape, and uniformed policemen stood watch all around. The title at the bottom of the screen, next to the network identification, read, "Brutal Murder in Palm Springs."

"The victim, as yet unidentified," said the offscreen anchor in a deep, professionally neutral baritone, "was found naked and beaten by a local man, who called the authorities immediately. She was pronounced dead at the scene. Police suspect she was sexually assaulted, and are beginning a canvas of the surrounding neighborhoods."

A brief flash of the victim's face appeared before the paramedics closed the ambulance doors. Young. Pretty. Though it was hard to be sure from all the bruising on her face from where her assailant had beaten her.

Jacob felt a surge of revulsion, followed be righteous indignation. What sort of a man would do that to a woman?

And how could Clara think *he* was to blame?

Jacob turned his gaze back to Clara and found her watching him with a knowing smirk.

"Repulsed? Shocked that something so horrible could happen and that I could blame you?"

He nodded.

She tapped the remote control again, and the display shifted.

Another news stream, this one dated three weeks after the first. The reporter, an olive-skinned woman with wavy black hair who wore a navy blue pants suit, stood in front of an official-looking building that was fronted by wide stairs and fluted columns. She spoke into a small microphone with practiced neutrality, though her eyes flashed - with satisfaction? - as she spoke.

"Breaking news about the serial killer that has been plaguing Palm Springs. Police today arrested a suspect in connection with the case. His identity has not been released, but officials say there is ample evidence to show that he stalked, raped, and then killed all seven victims."

Seven? Jacob shook his head and opened his mouth to speak, but the display shifted again and he lost his breath, and his stream of thought, in a heartbeat.

The video was from three days later.

"Donald Weatherby, the suspect in the Palm Springs killings, was denied bail today. The judge cited the extreme nature of the crimes and Weatherby's dismissive attitude in his decision. Weatherby was upbeat after the hearing."

"What do I care? I'll be out before long anyway," said another voice, one that sent shivers down Jacob's spine.

He wanted to look away, but he could not. He knew that voice; had known it his entire life.

He could have drawn the face of the smiling, joking man in correction-facility orange from memory.

The face was his own.

"What?" Jacob shook his head. "How?"

He did not do that. He could not have. And yet...

And yet there he was, plain as day.

"It's a trick. You..." He swallowed. "You doctored the video."

Clara shook her head slowly, her lips twisted into a little sneer of sadistic enjoyment, but she said nothing.

"Well that's not me!"

His shout evoked only another tap of her finger against the remote control.

The same female reporter from the earlier clip appeared on the display. This time she wore a loose-fitting blue dress that was elegant in its simplicity. In counterpoint to the neutral professionalism that Jacob had always heard reporters claim they had, she wore a broad smile and her eyes sparkled with...triumph?

"The jury has just announced its verdict in the Donald Weatherby trial, and it is unanimous: guilty on all counts. Sentencing is in two weeks. The District Attorney has announced he will push for a total memory wipe. The defense declined to comment."

The clip ended.

Jacob understood.

Oh God, it was true. He did not remember doing or saying any of those things because...

"It'd almost be more humane just to shoot him, you know?"

Lawrence's words, spoken all those weeks ago on the night Jacob and Clara first met - this time, anyway - rang in Jacob's ears. Or was it Donald? He still thought of himself as Jacob, but that was a lie, wasn't it? All his memories...what was real and what was a lie? How long had he really been here, living this life? Five years? No, the final clip had been from a year after his arrest. Four then? Two?

How long does it take to erase a man and create a new one within his own head?

He shook his head, part of himself trying to deny what was happening, but he could not. Oh Lord...he was a monster, and Lawrence was right. It would have been better if they had just put him down, all those years ago.

He was crying; he had not realized it before now, but his cheeks were wet with tears. His chest heaved and he felt the sobs wracking his chest, but it was almost as though it was another man doing it, not he.

And it really was another man, wasn't it?

Clara touched the remote control again, and a stream of pictures began flowing across the display. A young woman. Pretty, smiling, her auburn hair parted above her brows and hanging past her shoulders. Her hair done up in a bun. Cut short. Wearing a flowery summer dress. A graduation gown and cap. A brides-maid's dress.

Jacob did not have to ask; it was Clara's sister. What was her name? He should know it...

A final picture. The young woman, her face bruised, her nose broken, several teeth missing, her eyes open in the unfocused stare of death.

Jacob gagged and looked away, trying to keep his stomach contents down.

Clara bounded across the room and grabbed him by the hair. "Look at her," she growled, and forced his head around to face the display again.

Tears streamed down his cheeks again, and he sobbed.

"I'm..."

"*What?*"

Jacob swallowed and forced the sobs down. He opened his mouth, but all that came out was a whisper. "I'm sorry."

Clara released him, more like flung him away, and stepped back two paces. Her breathing was slow, steady, but her nostrils flared like a raging beast and there was a dreadful heat in her gaze.

"You're sorry." Her voice was flat, almost dead. She paused for a short moment, then shook her head. "Not good enough."

In the silence that followed, Jacob could clearly see, despite the ruined state of her face on the display, the family resemblance between Clara and her sister. It was an eery juxtaposition: Clara's life and vibrance next to her sister's silence and stillness. Jacob found he could not look away from the pair of them.

"What do you want from me?" He knew the answer, but he needed to hear her say it.

"They decided to wipe your memory, put in another. Send you to the other side of the world, where know one would know you, leave you here." Her sneer became a snarl. "My sister is dead, and you go on living as though nothing happened. And they call that justice."

She drew in a deep breath, then raised her right hand. Jacob had not even noticed she was still carrying the pistol.

"What do I want?" Clara said. "I want justice."

He should have been afraid. He should have cried out against the injustice of it all. But that would have been a lie. All he felt was resignation and somehow, perversely, relief. Lawrence was right, after all. All the same, he had to try.

"You know they'll catch you. Do the same as me. You won't remember her, me, you." He made a little gesture with his bound hands, taking in the room. "You won't even remember this. So what's the point?"

Clara stared at him for several seconds, then glanced off to her right. He turned his head and saw, over in the corner beside the directional lamp, a small camera. A red blinking light near its lens indicated it was recording.

"I'll remember," she said.

Then there was a flash, followed by the blackest darkness.

MEASURING UP

The camp was set up near a narrow river, in a wide field that allowed an easy line of sight for sentries to detect approaching visitors. Consisting of several hundred peaked tents, each large enough to house probably four or five men along with their equipment, and a single larger tent in the center, nearly a pavilion, no doubt for the commander and his staff, the camp was surrounded by an earthen wall behind a ditch that was filled with sharpened stakes to stave off an enemy's charge. There was but one point of ingress or egress readily visible, and that was guarded by a large wood and iron gate, and at least a dozen men who were easily visible. No doubt there were a number more who were hidden.

Larian reined in his horse, slowing to a walk as he approached the camp. A narrow wooden bridge spanned the ditch on the approach to the gate. It was a rickety-looking thing, and Larian suspected it was rigged to collapse in the face of an enemy onslaught. Though he was a novice at this game, it's what he would have done, so he had no doubt the camp's commander had thought of the same.

At the gate, a burly man in a shiny steel breastplate with an insignia of a swooping falcon before two crossed swords engraved in the breast, the emblem of the Citizens' Army, raised a hand, signaling Larian to stop. The man's face was only partially visible behind the vertical bars of his steel helm, but Larian could see a puckered scar on the man's forehead that split his left eyebrow. Suppressing a reflexive sympathetic cringe at the pain that wound must have caused, Larian obeyed without question.

"State your business," the guard said.

Larian fished inside his satchel for a moment, then produced a folded piece of paper, sealed with a wax stamp bearing the shield and spear of the Martial Academy at Tel Cerelon, and handed it to the guard.

"Larian Elesir reporting for duty, sir."

The guard looked the paper over, careful not to break the seal, and snorted.

"Don't call me sir, lad. I work for a living."

At a gesture from the guard, a pair of his companions behind the gate hauled on a rope, and the gate slowly began to rise. When it was fully open, the guard handed the paper back to Larian and waved him through.

"Check in with the Master Sergeant. Second tent on the left."

Larian nodded in thanks and heeled his horse forward. The camp was a bustle of activity. The loud clang of metal striking metal rang out from a forge off to the right. Messengers darted to and fro. Cooks and serving men cleaned up from the morning meal. Platoons mustered in formation for drill. All these things and more assaulted Larian's senses as he rode into the camp. The camp was almost a city unto itself, except for the marked lack of females.

The Master Sergeant's tent was larger than the others in its proximity, but not by much. A pair of horses were hitched at a post in front of the tent. Dismounting, Larian tied his gelding in place beside them, then ducked inside.

The man Larian presumed to be the Master Sergeant sat behind a folding desk near the entrance of the tent. A man stood at attention in front of the desk, with another behind him and to his right at parade rest. The man at attention was trembling visibly. Larian blanched as an onslaught of angry words reached his ears.

"...two weeks extra duty. And if I ever catch you sleeping on watch again, I'll make sure the Commander takes your head! Are we clear?"

The Master Sergeant's voice could have been Deus' himself, passing judgment at the Last Day, for the authority and disapproval it carried. The man at attention nodded quickly, his trembling growing greater by the second. With a disgusted gesture, the Master Sergeant waved him out, and the man at parade rest grabbed the trembling fellow by the arm and dragged him from the tent.

Alone in the tent now except for the Master Sergeant, Larian found himself the sole focus of the later's attention. Short-cut red hair, going grey about the ears, framed a hard face that was adorned by a tightly trimmed mustache and sharp green eyes. The Master Sergeant's uniform was impeccable: clean and neat, with every piece of metal polished to a mirror finish. Larian had to force himself not to wilt under the man's gaze.

"Right. Who are you then?"

Larian swallowed and produced his orders again. Holding them toward the Master Sergeant, he greeted him in the same manner he had the guard at the gate. The Master Sergeant took the orders and broke the seal, frowning as he read them through. Then, with a sigh, he looked back at Larian.

"Stand at ease, son," he said, his voice becoming, if not gentle, at least a bit less stern than he'd used with the last fellow. "Any trouble on your journey from the mainland?"

Larian shook his head. "No sir."

Another snort.

"I'm not an officer, son. My name is Master Sergeant Joran Hilbreth. Call me Master Sergeant, or just Top. Everyone else seems to. I answer only to the Commander. My job is to make sure you're taken care of while you're attached to this unit, and that you do your job properly." He smiled, a gap-toothed grin that didn't manage to make Larian feel any more comfortable. "Think of me as the uncle no one ever wanted to mess with, and we'll get along just fine."

Larian swallowed. "Yes, Master Sergeant."

The Master Sergeant chuckled softly, then returned his eyes to Larian's orders.

"Says here you were top in your class with the sword. Third with the bow. And that you're pretty good on a horse." He looked back up at Larian. "That so?"

Larian nodded, an eager grin coming to his face. "Yes, sir. Err...I mean, yes Master Sergeant. My horse is tied out front." He jerked his thumb toward the tent's opening.

"Good." The Master Sergeant set the orders down into a basket on the corner of his desk. Leaning back in his chair, he studied Larian for a long moment. "Have you ever been in a real fight, son? Ever killed a man?"

Larian hesitated. There was that incident with the brigands. But no, he'd promised himself never to mention that to anyone. He shook his head. "No, Master Sergeant."

"Hmph. Well, you'll soon get your chance. I'm assigning you to the B Company Scouts. They're heading out tomorrow to check out the area east of the river, so you'll have to get settled quickly."

Larian smiled with pleasure. He'd had his eye on a spot with the Scouts all through the Martial Academy. It seemed a far sight better than being an infantry grunt or, worse, an archer. So he'd pushed himself hard to meet their elevated entrance requirements.

The Master Sergeant, noticing his smile, stood from his chair and rounded the desk to stand in front of Larian.

"Don't be too happy, son. A Scout's life is hard, and there's a good chance it'll end in an unmarked grave. You ready to face that?"

"Yes, Master Sergeant."

He snorted again.

"We'll see about that. Come on, I was meaning to inspect B Company's messing this morning. I'll show you to the Leader of Scouts on the way."

Larian followed the Master Sergeant to the far side of the camp, leading his gelding by the bridle. The Master Sergeant explained as they walked that the camp was laid out by quarters, with each of the four Companies in the Regiment camped in one quarter. The camp had four main walkways leading to the command tent at the center, and secondary paths in concentric rings linking the four for easy access to any area. All horses, equipment, and supplies for each Company were kept near at hand, so even if one portion of the camp was breached, the others could mount an effective response.

B company was in the southeast corner, a walk of five minutes or so from the Master Sergeant's tent. When they arrived, the Company was just completing the morning muster, the various units dispersing to go about the day's work. The man the Master Sergeant approached was short and lean. He may once have been handsome, but the eyepatch over his left eye and the scar that puckered the same cheek prevented it now. The Master Sergeant cleared his throat and saluted, fist to heart.

The man returned the salute in kind, and greeted the Master Sergeant in a respectful tone.

"Morning, Master Sergeant. What can I do for you?"

"Got a new arrival for you, Lieutenant," he replied, gesturing toward Larian.

The Lieutenant's single eye turned toward the young man and, narrowing, took his measure quickly. He grunted.

"You're Yolath's replacement, huh? He was one of my best. Glad they didn't send us a total greenhorn to replace him." Larian blinked. He thought sure that was meant to be sarcastic, but the tone was completely serious. "Gerald!"

A nearby man, broad and muscular, with a merry twinkle in his eye, turned toward the Lieutenant and stepped forward.

"Yes sir?"

"Help Armsman..." he raised an eyebrow at Larian questioningly.

"Elesir, sir."

The Lieutenant continued. "Help Armsman Elesir get settled. I'll see you both at the ring in an hour."

Gerald saluted and replied, "Aye, sir." Then he gestured for Larian to follow him.

The Company's horse line was their first stop. It was located near the camp's wall, next to a fair-sized archery range. After logging in with the grooms, Larian tied his horse at the end of the line and hefted his belongings.

His tent was a short distance from the horse line, in a row shared by the other scouts. From the look of things, he shared it with three other men, though they were nowhere to be found when Larian and Gerald arrived.

"Just stack your gear in the corner for now," Gerald said as they surveyed the accommodations. "You need to check in with the quartermaster and get scheduled to see the Commander before we go to the ring. You'll have time to unpack this afternoon."

"What's the ring?"

Gerald grinned, the twinkle in his eye returning.

"Practice, lad. Practice."

"Ah. Why am I to see the Commander?"

"Standard Orders. Commander interviews every new man when he arrives in camp, and before he transfers to another unit or leaves the service."

"Really. Is that normal?"

Gerald shook his head. "No. The Commander is...unique. In a lot of ways. Won't find a better man anywhere, though."

That was encouraging. Larian had heard horror stories of bad COs during his time in the Martial Academy. From what he'd been able to gather, the quality of the CO had a huge impact, not just on whether a soldier survived his stint in the unit, but also on a soldier's quality of life, which was almost the more important of the two.

They found the Commander's assistant in the entry room to the central tent. He was brisk and efficient. Within moments of their arrival, Larian found himself scheduled for an interview that evening after dinner.

The quartermaster was not so efficient. It took most of the rest of their allotted hour to get Larian officially registered on the Regiment's roll and requisition his scout's kit. Larian had the uniform, armor, and sword he'd been issued at the Martial Academy, but he would need more than that. Eventually, they made it out of the quartermaster's tent with promises that his gear would be ready for pickup shortly after lunch.

Walking back to his Company's quadrant, Larian began to feel a bit anxious. He assumed that practice meant sparring, or something similar. He'd seen a lot of that at the Martial Academy, but it was different now that he was with his unit. He didn't want to put a foot wrong on his first day.

Gerald led him past the muster area and around a cluster of infantrymen's tents, easily identified by the the racks of long spears outside each tent. The two men rounded a corner in the walkway, and Larian saw the ring. It resided in a small clearing in the camp, maybe forty feet across. The ring itself was about twenty feet in diameter, and separated from the rest of the clearing by thin ropes strung between a series of posts that were dug into the earth.

A group of around thirty men waited in a loose gaggle in the clearing. The Lieutenant was addressing them as Larian and Gerald walked up.

"...Make sure you have your affairs in order, and your next of kin updated with the quartermaster. We leave at first light." The Lieutenant spied Larian and Gerald approaching and gestured Larian's way. "Here's the new man. Armsman Elesir is Yolath's replacement."

Every eye in the clearing turned toward Larian. He swallowed, wanting to squirm under the appraising stares of the more experienced men. But he managed to keep his back straight and nod in greeting to his new comrades.

"Got a first name, lad?" asked a grizzled man, older than most of the rest by a good ten years or more.

"Larian, sir."

A soft chuckle rippled through the gathered scouts as the man smirked. "I'm no sir, Elesir. Horace Mansfel, Platoon Sergeant."

He reached out to clasp hands with Larian, and that began a whirlwind of introductions. Every man in the unit said hello in a rush. Larian remembered maybe one name in three when it was all done, but he began to feel a bit better, more welcomed.

"Well, let's see what you're made of, Elesir," said the Lieutenant once introductions were done. "In the ring!"

The platoon spread out around the ring as Larian stepped beneath the rope boundary. On the far side of the ring from where he entered was a rack of practice swords: tightly bound bundles of bamboo that would leave a welt, but cause no real harm. Larian took a moment to pick out one that closely matched the balance of his own sword, then moved to the center of the ring.

"The Master Sergeant tells me that Elesir was top in his Academy class with the sword." The men had another collective chuckle at the Lieutenant's pronouncement. "Jiles, you're up."

Jiles, a lithe man who looked only a couple years older than Larian, slipped under the rope with an eager grin and fetched a sword of his own. Larian stepped back a pace to give him room near the center and assumed a ready stance, sword held loosely in both hands with the tip pointing at Jiles' eyes.

Jiles didn't bother settling into a stance, instead he came on in a rush. His sword seemed to dance, feinting left before cutting downward at Larian's head from above. Larian was taken by the feint, and had to lean back and pivot about his forward foot to avoid being struck. His riposte was weak, a quick upward cut that Jiles easily danced away from.

Sensing the advantage, Jiles attacked again, this time thrusting low toward the belly. Larian was better prepared for his speed the second time around. He spun his body completely around, parrying the thrust aside and countering with a neck-level cut at the completion of his spin. Jiles ducked into a roll to escape the cut, bounding to his feet with his back to Larian.

Larian advanced, reversing his swing and cutting downward at the back of Jiles' shoulder, where it joined the neck. But again Jiles was too quick, hopping to his right to avoid the cut and countering with a quick stab. Larian winced as the tip of Jiles' sword poked him in the side, just beneath his ribs.

"Up!" shouted the Lieutenant, and Jiles backed away, planting his sword tip into the dirt. Larian followed suit. Crestfallen, he lowered his gaze. So much for making a good impression.

"Not bad," said the Lieutenant, causing Larian to look up in surprise. The Lieutenant smirked slightly, adding, "Jiles is the best blade in the Platoon. Lasting three passes against him is not easy." With that, his gaze left Larian and moved to the rest of the men. "Thoughts?"

"That spin move looks fancy, but it leaves you wide open if there's another enemy around," Gerald offered. A chorus of agreement followed.

Jiles shook his head in disagreement. "It worked. Can't argue with results. His mistake was in assuming he had a free shot just because my back was turned. He committed too much to that attack, and couldn't recover in time."

"Agreed," said Sergeant Mansfel.

The Lieutenant nodded. "Right, then. Another pass."

And so it continued for the rest of the morning. Larian faced Jiles twice more, and lost to him both times. Then the Lieutenant rotated other men in. At first, he fared better, besting his opponents more often than not. But as the morning wore on, and he grew more and more tired. By the time the Lieutenant ended the session for lunch, Larian was soaked with sweat, breathing heavily. His arms and shoulders were like lead, and he bore a number of stinging welts all over his body. He'd never faced that many opponents, or sparred for such an extended period of time. He felt ready to collapse in a heap.

"That there is just a hint of what battle feels like," the Sergeant said as Larian stepped gingerly from the ring. "Course, in battle, there's no stopping for lunch. No stopping at all until the fight's done. Not if you want to live." He raised a meaningful eyebrow, then turned and walked away toward the mess tent.

Lunch itself was nothing special: a venison stew and hunks of bread, washed down with water. But it was boisterous, filled with conversation and good-natured joking between various members of the unit. Gerald set Larian down in the center of the table, and before long his comrades were peppering him with questions about his background. They were particularly eager to hear about Rosaline, his girl back home. That led to trouble.

He'd just finished describing her, when one of the other Scouts, a man named Harlan, quipped, "Sounds like a choice piece of ass there."

That struck too close to home. Larian recalled being tied, helplessly watching the brigand leader fondling her as he called her the same thing and promised to make Larian watch while he had his way. White-hot rage filled Larian, and he stood from the table, his fists clenched.

Conversation stopped. Harlan looked taken aback, then his eyes narrowed.

"You want to fight me, boy?"

"You take that back, right now, or..."

The Sergeant, sitting quietly at the end of the table, brought his fist down onto the table top hard enough to knock over several cups. The loud sound drew every eye as he rose from his chair.

Casting a baleful gaze on Larian, the Sergeant barked, "That's quite enough of that foolishness. Sit down, Larian. Now!"

Larian ground his teeth, but complied.

The Sergeant turned to Harlan and continued. "Harlan, you'd best apologize, and learn to guard your tongue."

Harlan glared at Larian for a long moment, then shrugged and said, "Sorry. Didn't mean nothing by it."

The rest of lunch was more subdued, or at least Larian enjoyed it less. He felt more than a little stupid about the whole incident. When they left, Harlan gave him a hard stare, but didn't say anything. Great. The last thing Larian needed was to make enemies here.

After lunch, Gerald led him back to the quartermaster, where he signed for and was issued the rest of his gear. Then it was back to his tent, where he met the men he'd be bunking with. To his surprise, Jiles was one of them. The others were a Hern, muscle-bound and blond, with a huge nose that didn't fit his face, and Paoli, who was quite possibly the tallest man Larian had ever seen. All three seemed good-natured, and welcomed him with grins as he unpacked his gear.

The three of them, along with Gerald, spent most of the after-noon teaching Larian some of the specialized tools and techniques the Scouts used. In the Martial Academy, he had learned basic hand-signals that all soldiers used.

But the Scouts had an entirely separate vocabulary of gestures. Simple, yes, but there were many of them. By mid-afternoon Larian had a few of them down, but he was far from confident with what he'd learned. Then there was the cipher, and the care of pigeons. His comrades explained that every Scout unit travelled with a number of them, in case the unit found information that needed to get to the Commander immediately. The cipher was specially developed for writing those messages, and Larian was expected to memorize it.

Between those two new topics, he began to feel overwhelmed, and said so. His comrades reassured him, though, that he wasn't expected to know it all immediately. It would be months before the Sergeant or the Lieutenant would task him with writing a message. All the same, he would be expected to study each day, and log his study time with the Sergeant, until he had mastered both the cipher and the gesture language.

Dinner was much like lunch, even down to the food, except there was ale instead of water. When dinner was over, Gerald led him back to the Commander's tent. The assistant greeted him with a grunt, then waved him into a chair to wait for the Commander's summons. Gerald clapped him on the shoulder, then left to see to other duties, and Larian sat down.

Fifteen minutes passed, then four men in officers' uniforms stepped through the tent flap leading into the main area of the tent. Larian stood quickly, coming to attention, but the men didn't notice him, engrossed in conversation among themselves as they were. A moment later, they were gone, and another man stepped into the entry room. Of average height, with thinning black hair and a slight build, he wore a simple soldier's uniform, indistinguishable from Larian's own except for a golden epaulette on the man's right shoulder.

"Anything else tonight, Tomi?" asked the man.

The assistant gestured toward Larian. "Armsman Elesir is here for his check-in interview, Commander."

"Oh yes, our new Scout." The Commander looked Larian over for a moment, then said, "Come on in, son."

Larian followed him into the next room. Well appointed, with rich carpeting on the floors, a sturdy desk along one wall, a number of folding chairs around the periphery, and a medium-sized table that was covered in maps and other documents in the center of the room, it was a place of business, not of leisure. The Commander sat down behind his desk and gestured for Larian to sit as well. He obeyed, pulling one of the folding chairs over in front of the desk.

"It's Larian, isn't it?"

He nodded.

"Well, Larian, I hear from Lieutenant Pallak that you're cunning with a sword and have the endurance of an ox. High praise, coming from him."

Larian blinked in surprise at the unexpected compliment. The Commander chuckled, no doubt seeing the surprise on his face.

"You'll find the Lieutenant is sparing in praise, but you'll know it when he doesn't approve of what you've done." The Commander clasped his hands together atop the desk and leaned forward, peering into Larian's eyes intently. "Now then, why are you here?"

"There's a war on, sir. It's my duty...."

The Commander snorted loudly. "Your little village never had dealings with the Mar Tabban, and probably never will. So why did you come halfway across creation to fight a war that won't affect your home?"

"The nation is my home, sir, not just my village."

"Yes, yes. But that's not why you're here, is it?"

"Sir, I don't..."

"You're here for adventure. Maybe a hint of glory, eh?"

"I suppose maybe that had crossed my mind."

"Of course it did. All young men feel that same call." The Commander pointed a finger at him as he continued. "But there's no room for that here. Go off seeking glory and excitement in this business, and you'll end up dead. You can't afford that, and neither can I. I expect a lot of my Scouts. You are my eyes and ears out there, and this Regiment will live or die based on the information you bring, or fail to bring. So I need you to be on the ball and professional at all times, understand?"

Larian nodded hurriedly.

"Good. Now then, tell me about yourself."

For the next twenty minutes or so, the conversation centered on Larian's past: his home village, his parents, Rosaline, his time at the Martial Academy. The Commander was very engaging and seemed genuinely interested in Larian's story, so he found himself telling more than he expected. He held back from talking about the Brigands again; it was just a bit too embarrassing a tale. Finally, the Commander glanced at a small clock - a CLOCK - on his desk, and grunted.

"Well it's starting to get late. You've had a busy day, and tomorrow's shaping up to be busier. The General Staff thinks those Mar Tabban bastards are going to move into our sector soon. If that's true, I'll need you and your unit at your best. Go get some rest."

Larian stood and saluted. "Thank you for your time, sir."

"Thank *you*. I'm honored to serve with you under my command. Do me proud out there, son."

Larian walked out of the tent, feeling a mile tall. Gerald was right: the Commander was a great man, and Larian felt fortunate to be in his unit.

Back at his unit's camp, he found his tentmates, as well as a few other men, engaged in a game of dice around the fire. Jiles waved him over to join in, but Larian refused with a polite smile. It had been a long day, and he was exhausted. Stepping into the tent, he stripped down to his small clothes and slid into his bedroll. He remained awake for a while, his thoughts drifting to the next day. He suppressed a mixture of excitement and anxiety over their mission. It would be what it would be, but for the time being, he was content that he was in a good place. His last thought as he drifted off to sleep was to wonder what Rosaline was doing, and to make a short prayer to Deus that he would survive the war to see her again.

A CHAT BEFORE DINNER

I t's a hard life, being a zombie.

No, really. You try one day finding yourself craving, not that awesome filet from the local steakhouse, but a nice flank cut from the neighbor down the street. Let me tell you, the steakhouse filet tastes much better.

So why not stick with that? Why go the human route?

Believe me, I tried, but there's just something more satisfying about man flesh. I suppose you could say it's an acquired taste.

But not just any hunk of human will do.

At first, I tried just going to the morgue, but that about killed me. Yeah, bad pun I know. But seriously, that cold, dead meat just played havoc with my guts. And if, God forbid, they've already started the embalming process? Formaldehyde is NOT a pleasant taste at all, and it burns going down. Better to starve.

No, fresh warm human is the way to go.

Of course, everyone has their own taste in this matter. This guy I know over in Rock Hills Cemetery loves it really rare. If it ain't still kicking, I don't eat it, he says.

But me, I prefer it more on the medium side. Right on the edge of passing on, but not completely dead yet. It gives the meat a little extra zip, if you know what I mean.

Now, my girl, she won't touch it until it's fully dead. Says she doesn't like it too bloody. I guess I can understand that.

But no one, and I mean no one, will eat it after it's gone totally cold.

Do I feel bad about it? Sure, sometimes. A lot more at first than I do now, of course. Every so often though, I'll be eating some hot broad, and a part of me will realize, hey, she's actually HOT.

Or she would be, if I still looked at humans that way.

I mean really, I'm no pervert here, but I remember how it was back before I changed. Sometimes part of me regrets depriving some human fellow of the pleasure of her company.

It only lasts a second, of course. I mean, you might feel bad for eating a deer or a cow for a short while, but you don't dwell on it. Survival of the fittest, the natural order, right? It's no different with me.

What's that you say? It's NOT part of the natural order? Well, let me get to that in a second.

The other bad part about zombie life is, of course, the accommodations. I mean really. Crypts, sarcophagi, open graves...these are not fun places to hang out.

The vampires though, man, those guys have it made. They've got their own mausoleums, plush felt-lined coffins, human minions and guard dogs.

Do we get any of that? Hell no.

Just try convincing a human that it would be glamorous to get turned into a zombie and see what how he reacts. Being laughed at like that is NOT good for the ego, let me tell you. But somehow those vamps have humans lining up like sheep for a shot at the prize.

Stupid fleshlings don't know what they're missing.

And of course, Dracula and his boys are always rubbing it in our faces too.

I tell you, it's a conspiracy. The man just goes out of his way to keep us zombies down. Well, we're not gonna take it forever. One of these days, the rank and file of the undead world is gonna rise up, and ol' Vlaad will WISH he'd shown us more respect. Just you wait.

But getting back to my point, it gets freaking cold in those places, man. And it's wet. Plus, there's bugs out the wazoo. And sometimes in the wazoo, too. Let me tell you, THAT is uncomfortable. And a bit gross, to be perfectly frank.

Speaking of gross, that brings up another annoying thing about zombie life. It gets really tiresome to have little bits and pieces fall off.

Yeah, yeah, I know. We're walking corpses. We rot. But what you humans don't know is we also grow back. It's this tiring cycle of rot, fall off, grow back. Rot, fall off, grow back. Over and over and over again.

I could accept it if all I did was slowly rot away. Hell, back when I was human that's all I was really doing anyway. It was just on a longer time scale than your typical zombie rot.

But now, I go through a whole set of skin every week or so, and my other soft tissues, about every month. It makes it really hard to pick up the zombie chicks when your tongue falls out of your mouth.

I lost out on two prime catches that way.

I mean, we all lose parts every day or so. Did I complain when Sheila's ear fell off into my food? Hell no! But man I lose one pound of flesh and she says I'm going to turn into a skeleton if I don't take better care of myself.

You believe that? A skeleton! Those dudes ain't got nothing on me, man!

I tried to tell her that, but she just gave me the finger...literally...and stormed off.

I hear she's with JuJu down by the old dungeon now. That condescending prick. Just cause he was a prize fighter or whatever back before he changed, and managed to stay fast and strong, while the rest of us hobble around all day...

Whatever.

Fortunately, my current girl is more understanding than the

others, and I'm very happy with her. She appreciates me for who and what I am.

Which I guess brings me back to your little question. It's appropriate, I guess, since it illustrates the single worst part about being a zombie: having to deal with the constant, unending bigotry from you humans.

Maybe it's just your way of dealing with your inferiority. I guess I can understand that. You are, after all, our prey. It must make you feel insecure.

But really, just because we tend to shamble around doesn't mean we're weaklings. And just because sometimes our vocal chords have rotted out and the only sound we can make is a pathetic groan doesn't mean we're stupid.

Sheesh, my roommate was a PhD, for Christ's sake!

I mean really, if you let him, he'll talk your ear off, literally, about the intricacies of quantum mechanics, and the leading theories on how to merge it with relativity, or some such. I dunno much about all that, but I'm telling you that guy's smart. And he can cook, too.

Look, I understand how stereotypes get started, and that they all have some basis in truth, however small. But seriously folks, would it kill you to sit down and talk with an average zombie BEFORE making a movie about us?

Ok, I guess it would. Probably.

But that's not the point.

I mean, where do you guys *get* this shit? Seriously, brains? Brains? Who the hell goes stumbling around with their arms stretched out in front of them, moaning "brains" all day? And who the hell actually *eats* brains? No one I've ever met.

Really folks, it's called research. It would take all of five minutes to learn this stuff.

But then you guys can't seem to do the minimal research it would take to learn that spy satellites are not in geosynchronous orbit over the United States, or anywhere else for that matter. Do you have any idea how high geosynchronous orbit is? Good luck getting good pictures from there, dude.

And while I'm on the subject, you just can't get real time video, complete with thermal imaging, off them. Neither can any jackass cop just call a Navy Lieutenant to get data from one of these satellites whenever he feels like it, just because he happens to be the bad-ass ex-SEAL she's banging, so he can get a nice deus ex machina assist in solving the case that's stumped him for the last forty-five minutes of prime time television. He especially can't call her from a cell phone and expect to get an answer when she's deep inside CIC on an aircraft carrier.

Way the hell out at sea.

Seriously? Where the hell do you think the cell towers are for that signal? Sheesh, you freaking humans.

See, it's that kind of stupidity and laziness that pisses me off and makes the movies you people try to make about us suck so bad. Really. Do your homework for a change, people!

Wow, I didn't plan to go off on a rant. Sorry about that.

But getting back to it, if all we had to deal with from your racism was bad movies, I wouldn't really complain. I mean, I like a bad zombie flick as much as the next guy. Hell, me and my buds have gotten many a good laugh from Night of the Living Dead (probably for different reasons than you do).

But no, we also have to deal with all those asshole zombie hunter wannabes.

Here's where I get back to the whole natural order bit. And I'm being serious here. Do some cows decide they're going to hunt humans for a change? Some lambs or goats? How about chickens, do they ever come hunting you? No? Ever wondered to ask why?

I'll tell you why: the natural order.

They eat what they eat. You eat them. It's called the food chain, people. I think it's covered in elementary school. So where do you get off thinking it's ok to come hunting us?

What's that? Self defense? Yeah right.

Ok look, if I'm taking a human down, and he turns and

whacks me instead, he's a) very very impressive, b) probably not really human, and c) legitimately defending himself.

But that's not what I'm talking about. I'm talking about some jackoff who gets a bunch of gear and comes trying to hunt ME down. How does that become ok and in keeping with the natural plan?

Don't go off on that whole "Zombies aren't part of the natural order" bit. That's totally racist. And also patently untrue from even the most cursory of examinations. There have been zombies for as long as there have been humans. Vampires, werewolves, and walking skeletons too.

But really, don't put those last guys in the same category as the rest of us. They're really quite embarrassingly pathetic, truth be told.

Might as well claim all those guys aren't part of the natural order either. But since they are, you really can't say zombies aren't. Quod erat demonstrandum, my friend.

What? You say they're not natural either? Dude, have you even listened to anything I've been saying for the last few minutes? You really are irretrievably dense aren't you?

But anyway, getting back to these zombie hunters. It would be one thing if they were actually serious, but they're not. And that's the most insulting thing about them: they come completely unprepared.

I suppose maybe they think they're ready to rumble in their minds, tiny though they may be. But I've yet to meet or hear of one who didn't show up looking like he'd taken his cues from the worst of the bad Hollywood zombie flicks. At best. Some of these schmucks show up with garlic and crucifixes, for Christ's sake! I mean, seriously? That shit doesn't even really work on vampires, let alone on us.

Pathetic.

And then you've got the morons who come packing heat. Sometimes they think they're really being clever by loading silver bullets.

Woooo! I'm really scared! Hey jackass, I'm a fricking walking corpse! A lot of good shooting me is going to do you! Might as well hit me with a pillow!

Interestingly enough, this one guy did that a couple weeks back. He actually came the closest to getting away of anyone in the last year. It helped his cause that one of my eyes had rotted out earlier that day, but the pillow was actually quite effective at tripping me up. If he'd been in shape, as opposed to being a blubber butt, he might have made it. But in the end, it didn't matter.

Mmm, that was some nice, tender meat.

Where was I? Oh yes, the douchebags with guns.

I tell you, man, I must have encountered a half dozen guys like that in the last year. Each and every one had the same stupid, confused look on his face when I started eating him, like he couldn't understand how his careful Hollywood research failed him.

You know, I told you before that I don't care for meat that's too rare, but for those idiots, I made an exception.

So what's the right way to kill a zombie then?

Wouldn't you like to know. Who do you think I am, Ernst Stavro Blofeld to your James Bond? I'm not just going to tell you the whole plot, secure in my superiority and the fact that you'll be dead in a few minutes, so what can it hurt.

No, that's something you'll have to learn the hard way. If you get the chance. Which, as I just mentioned, you won't.

So anyway, I've really enjoyed this little chat, but my girl's going to be here in a few minutes, and like I told you she prefers her meat fully dead. So I'm afraid I need to start getting things ready.

What's that?

Oh come on now. You're really just embarrassing yourself. Hell, if you keep it up I'll be embarrassed *for* you.

There's this little thing called meeting your end with dignity, my man. Didn't your dad ever teach you about that? Fighting to the end, not giving the bastards the satisfaction, all that?

Oh, you never met him, huh. Well, sorry about that. If it's any consolation, my folks split up when I was two, so I was never all that close with my dad either.

What are you looking at?

Oh! Hey babe, I didn't hear you come in. Sorry, I'm running a little behind tonight. Dinner will be ready in just a moment.

Can I get you a drink? Ok, well make yourself comfortable.

Quite a looker, eh my man?

Hmmph. Well no offense, but I saw your little squeeze earlier and she's not much to talk about at all. NO meat on those bones. How do you have any fun with a girl like that? Aren't you afraid you'll break her?

Oh well, it's a moot point now, I guess. Better get to it.

Hey, stop squirming! This will hurt a lot less if you just hold still.

FIRST BLOOD

The sound of a morning dove pierced the silence of the woods, making Larian smile slightly. He always loved birds - their colors, their songs, their grace in flight. For a short time, he let his thoughts wander and considered how wondrous it would be to soar through the sky as they did. Such joy they must feel.

"Elesir!"

Sergeant Mansfel's harsh whisper brought Larian back to the present. He started slightly and glanced aside toward the Sergeant, wincing apologetically. The Sergeant scowled and and pointed his first two fingers at his eyes then toward the area to Larian's right. Larian followed the Sergeant's fingers with his gaze and cursed under his breath.

The two men were perched in a tree at the edge of a clearing, twenty feet up. Above their thick leather armor, they wore cloaks patterned in greys, browns, and greens to blend in with the natural surroundings. The Sergeant had chosen their position with care. It offered clear views in three directions. Any of the enemy who came through would be easy to spot.

Which is why Larian should have been the first to see the troupe marching through the clearing to his right. If he had not been daydreaming, that is. He shook his head in chagrin, cursing himself for his inattentiveness. Then he nodded and began counting.

Twenty. Fifty. A hundred. One-fifty. A full company and more passed their tree, not a hundred feet distant.

He glanced at the Sergeant as the enemy force's rear guard vanished into the woods behind them. The grizzled warrior rolled his eyes and pointed at himself then the limb below, where their caged pigeons sat. Then he pointed at Larian and made a writing gesture. Larian nodded and pulled a piece of charcoal and a paper from his tool pouch.

The Sergeant slipped down to the pigeon cage and Larian began writing. He still felt uncertain with the scouts' cipher, despite weeks of practice every day. All the same, he got the details of what they saw written down quickly. By the time the Sergeant returned, pigeon clutched tightly in his hand, Larian finished reading through what he had written. He nodded in satisfaction then showed it to the Sergeant. The older man's eyes scanned the page briefly, then he nodded, smiling ever so slightly in approval.

A minute later, the Sergeant released the pigeon, the report carefully rolled up into a case around its neck. The bird flapped its wings and quickly gained altitude, then turned and headed away behind the two men and to their left.

Back in that direction, several miles away - fifteen, maybe twenty - lay their Regiment's forward encampment. Larian's platoon, the scouts of B Company, had departed base camp two weeks earlier. The Commander had received word through intelligence that the Mar Tabban were planning a raid through the Regiment's assigned territory and ordered the scouts to investigate. They had found enough hints to make the Commander put the Regiment on alert, but nothing definitive. Three days ago, he sent the scouts out again.

This was the first real contact with the enemy beyond signs and rumor. Larian felt a rush of excitement coupled with a tingling in his limbs as adrenalin took hold. He tried not to remember that just a moment ago he had nearly wet himself when he first saw the enemy soldiers marching in column. That was not the sort of thing a man, and a soldier to boot, did.

Good thing he had managed to keep himself under control. He would never live *that* down.

The two men waited for nearly an hour, but no more enemy troops came within observation of their position. Either there were no more or the enemy commander had decided to divide his men up to make them harder to detect. Larian suspected the latter. But then, he was very new to this, so what did he know?

Finally, the Sergeant cleared his throat, drawing Larian's attention to himself, then pointed down toward the ground. Larian looked up at the sun, now well past its zenith, and nodded. Moving quickly, but with care to avoid making too much noise, they descended from their perch to the ground below.

"Now what?" Larian whispered.

The Sergeant looked around carefully then leaned in close. "Now," he said in a whisper that barely carried to Larian's ears despite the other man's proximity, "we go to the rally point. Lieutenant will want to know about this."

Larian nodded. The pigeons were trained to return to the coop at the regimental camp; the Lieutenant would not receive the message that way.

The Sergeant gestured for Larian to follow and moved away at a quick but careful pace.

The hardest part of keeping up with him was avoiding twigs, branches, bushes, and other objects that would make excessive sound and give away their position. Larian had been learning, but he was still new to this and found it difficult. The Sergeant's gait, on the other hand, was apparently effortless. He moved through brush, grass, or across stone with the same lack of sound, hardly leaving a trace of his passage at all.

Which was, Larian supposed, the reason he found himself teamed up with the Sergeant more often than not. The most experienced enlisted armsman in the platoon, the Sergeant made it his business to make sure that everyone was up to snuff. Maybe because that was his job, Larian reminded himself whenever he got annoyed with the extra attention.

This day, though, Larian was not upset at being nurse-maided. Not anymore. The Mar Tabban were really here; suddenly the soldier act was no longer just an act. It was real, and deadly serious.

The rally point was next to a small outcropping of rock, two miles distant from the clearing Larian and the Sergeant had been staking out. The Lieutenant had picked it because of its location, practically in the center of the small valley the scouts were checking this day, which made it relatively easy to find.

It was not until he and the Sergeant were drawing near to it that Larian realized that if they could find it easily, the enemy could as well. He drew up short, suddenly uncertain.

The Sergeant continued on several paces before he noticed that Larian had stopped. He turned and looked back at Larian, his expression questioning, then he crept back within earshot of a low whisper.

"What's wrong, Elesir?"

"Nothing. It's just..." Larian paused, feeling foolish for some reason. He looked away from the Sergeant's gaze and flushed.

"What?" The Sergeant's voice was insistent.

"How do we know the Mar Tabban haven't found this place already?"

The Sergeant's eyebrows lifted high on his head. "Getting a little jumpy, aren't you?" He shook his head and grinned. "This is our land; we know the terrain here better than they." He clapped Larian lightly on the shoulder and gave it a quick squeeze. "Come on."

Larian grinned in return and, casting his doubts aside, followed the Sergeant up to the rock.

The rock jutted out from the side of a low hill near its crest. The trees thinned out around the rock, which looked almost like a single curved claw of some giant beast thrusting out of the earth. As the two men stepped out into the clearing below it, Larian could see no other men around.

"We must be the first," the Sergeant murmured. Then he whistled, his gruff voice mimicking a bluejay's call perfectly. After half a minute with no response, he tried again with the same result. Then he shrugged and stepped up toward the rock and removed his helmet.

"I guess we wait," he said.

A sudden movement in the undergrowth to the left, beyond the Sergeant's shoulder, drew Larian's attention. His eyes widened as he saw a figure in browns and greens level a bow and draw back on the string.

"Down!" Larian cried and threw himself atop the Sergeant, bearing him to the ground at the same time the archer released the bowstring with a sharp 'Twang'.

The two men hit the ground, the wind leaving the Sergeant's lungs in a loud exhalation. Larian cringed as the loosed arrow passed above them; he felt the movement of the air in its wake, it was so close!

A curse from the archer's direction reminded Larian that this was no time to cower. He rolled off the Sergeant then sprung his feet and drew his sword in one smooth motion. And was greeted by two men in dark leather armor, wearing cloaks of green and brown that were cut in an unfamiliar, foreign manner. They advanced from the vicinity of the archer's location. Larian did not need to see their bared blades to know they were the enemy.

The pair paused for a moment, looking at Larian warily as though surprised or intimidated. Larian scoffed inwardly. Intimidated? By what? Him? That was to laugh.

By the time the thoughts flashed through Larian's mind, the two men overcame whatever it was that stopped them. They glanced at each other and advanced, moving apart as they came so that they would be at his flanks by the time they closed the distance.

Behind him, Larian heard the Sergeant trying to rise, but he was gasping loudly as he struggled to regain his breath. He would not be ready to fight for a few moments. Larian would have to face the two men on his own, for now. And the archer, wherever he was. Larian spared a glance toward the area where he last stood, but could see no sign.

The two swordsmen came nearer. Larian licked his lips and fought to suppress a surge of fear. His mouth went dry and he could hear his heart pounding in his ears. A loud voice within screamed at him, "Run! These men are more experienced than you! You are a dead man if you stay!" He tried to tell the voice to shut up, but it just shouted all the louder.

Larian backed up a half step. The swordsman to his right grinned, a malicious smile of triumph, as the other man perceived Larian's fear. It was the man to his left, though, who came first. Without even a whisper of a battle cry, the man raised his sword and advanced, cutting downward and to the left toward the back of Larian's neck.

Larian moved without thinking, months of training spurring his muscles into motion despite his continuing doubt. He leapt to his left and swung his sword. His blade met his attacker's with a loud clang, but he did not stop there. He pivoted around his forward foot and spun around completely, his left elbow leading the way as he landed on his attacker's left side.

Larian heard as much as felt when his elbow connected with the side of the man's face. The man let out a grunt of surprise and pain in time with a crunching sound as either the bone of his cheek or several teeth broke. Larian continued his spin, letting his momentum carry in behind the man. He landed on his right foot and turned to face the man's back, bringing his blade down in a descending arc.

The man let out another cry, this one more high-pitched, as Larian's sword cut through his left boot and into the meat of his calf. He fell to the ground, clutching at his wounds and thrashing around in pain.

Larian came to a halt, amazed at what had just happened. He glanced down at the fallen man, then up at his sword, now stained red on the last few inches of its blade. A small drop of blood pooled and fell from the tip, and Larian swallowed again.

The second swordsman paused as well, his eyes growing wide with what Larian could only hope was fear. Then the other man took a breath and his eyes narrowed. He advanced, more slowly this time. Larian rolled his shoulders to loosen them and laid his left hand below his right on the hand-and-a-half hilt of his sword. Then, stepping carefully to give the fallen man a wide berth, he moved forward to meet the oncoming swordsman.

The swordsman came forward with quick, controlled steps. His attack was a measured thrust, not the all-out approach his fellow had taken, which Larian was able to sidestep with ease. It flashed through Larian's mind that it could not be this easy as he cut downward at the man's neck, where it met his shoulder. He gritted his teeth in anticipation of the impact.

But his attack never landed. The man recovered from his thrust faster than Larian would have thought possible and brought his blade up across his body to deflect Larian's cut off to the side.

Larian lurched forward, thrown off-balance by the unexpected parry. He could not afford to fall but it seemed inevitable, so he pushed himself forward, hitting the ground and rolling over his shoulders before springing back to his feet.

He felt as much as heard the man approaching from behind. He was right handed so he would probably cut from that side... Flashing back to his time in the ring with Jiles, Larian leapt to his right and spun to face his opponent.

Sure enough, the man's sword swept through empty air where Larian's back used to be and it was his turn to stumble forward. Larian again moved without thought, stepping forward and thrusting his blade into the man's armpit. The sword slid in far more easily than Larian would have expected.

The man stiffened, his eyes widening in shock and sudden pain, then let out a long gurgling groan. The sword fell from his hand, landing on the rocky ground with a metallic clank. The man turned his head and looked Larian in the eye. His gaze was not hate-filled, as Larian would have expect from one of the Mar Tabban. Instead, it was almost warm. The corners of the man's mouth turned upward slightly and his lips parted as if to say something. But then his eyes went vacant, losing their focus, and he slumped forward limply.

The body slid off of Larian's blade and landed on the ground with a soft thud.

A harsh cry to his right brought Larian spinning around, his sword raised to en garde. And saw the archer stumble into the clearing from behind a tree. He grasped at his belly, which was cut open from hip to hip, trying in vain to keep his innards from spilling out. His stumbling feet caught on a rock and he fell to the ground face-first.

"He'll be done in a moment," said the Sergeant as he stepped into view from behind the same tree. He wiped blood from the steel of his blade and looked from Larian to the two downed swordsman. "Is that one going to live?" He nodded at the first man Larian had felled.

Larian nodded. "I got him in the leg is all."

"Excellent." The Sergeant sheathed his sword and strode over to the stricken man, a grimly satisfied expression on his face. "Prisoners are always..."

He broke off suddenly, cocking his head to the side.

"What..."

The Sergeant put one finger to his lips then ducked behind the rock outcropping, gesturing for Larian to do so as well. Larian joined him there and they waited.

It was all Larian could do to not rush out to meet whatever had the Sergeant worried straight on. He tingled all over, felt supercharged. A small voice in the back of his head whispered it was just a battle high, that he needed to remain calm and still. But oh, it was difficult. He just wanted to run and smite something!

The seconds passed like hours, with Larian wondering how much longer he could stand to wait. Then, with a series of quiet rustles, a quartet of men in cowled cloaks of greys, browns, and greens bolted from the trees on either side of the clearing, bared weapons gleaming in the early afternoon sunlight.

The tension in the Sergeant's shoulders slid away and he exhaled softly. Glancing at Larian, he shook his head, in relief Larian thought, then stepped around the rock into the open.

"Ho there, Lieutenant," called the Sergeant.

The four men spun in unison, their cloaks flowing around them like fans as they turned toward the Sergeant and raised their weapons. Then, just as quickly, they lowered the weapons and relaxed. The men pushed back their cowls, revealing familiar faces. The man in the middle, shorter than the others by a hand, had a rugged face framed with black hair. His left eye was covered by an eyepatch and a puckered scar ran down the same cheek.

Lieutenant Pallak nodded to the Sergeant, then to Larian as he too stepped into view. Gesturing at the fallen men, he raised an eyebrow. "We heard sounds of a fight. Glad to see you had things in hand."

The Sergeant shrugged. "Elesir did most of the damage, sir." He related what had occurred and walked over to the wounded man, who by then had stopped thrashing and looked at the assembled scouts with defiance laced heavily with fear. "Scouts from the look of them. Had the same idea we did, I s'pose."

The Lieutenant nodded then gestured to the Sergeant and two of the men at his side. "Set up a perimeter. We don't want to get caught by surprise."

They nodded and fanned out into the woods. Faint sounds carried to Larian's ears as they took perches in trees around the clearing.

"Get that man ready to travel," the Lieutenant said to Larian and the other man in the clearing, Larian's tent-mate Jiles. "You two are bringing him back to base. Command is going to want to talk to him."

Over the next several minutes, Larian and Jiles first disarmed then searched and tied up the wounded Mar Tabban scout. Once certain he was no longer a threat, they cleaned and bound the cut to his calf, then helped him to his feet. Jiles found a good-sized stick that could pass for a crutch. After a brief discussion, they decided to modify his bonds so he could use the crutch to walk. They tied his left hand to the haft of the crutch and fashioned a lasso around the end of it to keep it tucked into his shoulder. His right hand they tied behind his back by itself. Possibly he could take a swing at one of them with the crutch, but what would that gain him? Larian would not try that if he were in the fellow's position, and he doubted the prisoner would either.

By the time they had the man ready to go, the rest of the scouts from Larian's platoon arrived at the rock outcropping. The Lieutenant filled them in on what happened there and they all compared notes on what they had seen that day. It all added up to a sizable Mar Tabban force - at least four companies of soldiers, but probably more. Larian had to fight down a surge of anxiety as they tallied up the numbers; their own regiment only consisted of four companies and being outnumbered was never a good position to be in.

Then it was time for Larian and Jiles to get going with their prisoner. The others in the platoon clapped them on their shoulders and wished them luck, then stepped back so the Lieutenant could have his say.

"Move quickly; do not stop for the night," he ordered. "Drop him off as soon as you can, then get back out here." He paused and took a deep breath. "But above all, be safe. Good luck."

They followed the Lieutenant's orders to the letter, not stopping at all except for very brief meals and for the call of nature. It was slow going with their prisoner, and at every turn Larian half expected to run into a column of Mar Tabban soldiers. But whether by luck or through Deus' good will, they encountered no one until mid-morning the next day when they came upon the outer pickets from Regimental headquarters.

As they passed the pickets by and walked the last mile to the camp, Larian felt a large tension that he had not even realized he was carrying fall away. Later on that day, he would likely be out again and in danger. But he had met the enemy in combat for the first time and come out, not just alive, but victorious. And for now, at least, he was safe. It was a good day.

WHO ATE MY SOCK?

"Another mismatched sock," Justine's mother muttered in irritation. Her face was set in an annoyed expression. For a few seconds, she pawed through the small pile of clothes sitting next to her on the floor. Coming up empty, she blew a dangling lock of hair away from her face with a snort and tossed the single sock in her hand into the laundry basket to her side.

"How the hell do we keep losing socks?," she asked the air in the living room.

Justine shrugged and picked up a shirt from the pile of laundry and began to fold it. Every wash, it seemed, her mother complained about the same thing. There was always a missing sock. Never mind that the socks turned up most of the time; they were in the next load, or she found them in the space between the washer and dryer, shriveled and stiff from having dried in the chilly dampness of the basement instead of the warmth of the clothes dryer. But Mom grumbled anyway. Justine suspected it gave her a certain satisfaction, as though grumbling about this little thing helped her cope with the other mundane annoyances of life.

Justine smiled to herself. If that was what helped keep Mom happy, she was all for it.

"I keep telling you, Linda. The dryer is a trans-dimensional vortex that sucks socks away at random," said Justine's Dad from behind her. He punctuated his words with a warm chuckle. Justine was certain he winked at her Mom too. That was a long-running gag between them.

This afternoon, though, Mom was having none of it. She glared at Dad and said between gritted teeth, "Shut up, Henry. Really!" She pointedly looked away from him and snatched up a pair of pants, then set about folding them in a quite violent manner.

Justine blinked, confusion and a bit of apprehension growing within her. Why the tension all of a sudden? Mom was acting affronted, but it was not like Dad had done anything wrong. Had he? She looked back at him over her shoulder. He was sitting at the table, reading the paper like always. Mom was not mad at him for not helping with the laundry; Justine remembered the one time he tried to help. He had made such a mess of folding that Mom actually banned him from laundry duty. He had actually looked stricken.

No answers were forthcoming so Justine went about her business helping Mom fold the clothes. They worked in silence for the next five minutes, thankfully finding no more missing socks. Then Mom stood up and hefted the laundry basket, full of neatly folded items of clothing. Mom turned and walked toward the stairs leading up to the bedrooms. But when she reached the bottom of the stairs, she stopped and muttered what sounded like a curse under her breath.

She looked back at Justine and said more loudly, "Justine dear, I forgot to move the laundry from the washer to the dryer. Would you go do that for me?"

Justine swallowed down a bit of nervous tension and nodded. "Yes, Mom," she said.

Mom smiled thankfully and proceeded up the stairs and out of sight.

Justine pushed herself to her feet and smoothed out the summer skirt she was wearing. She shivered, but not from nerves. It was the air conditioning. Her parents had set it too low. She was *not* afraid to go down into the basement! That was a child's fear and she was not a little girl any more!

But when she turned around, she found she had to force herself to make each step toward the door leading down into the basement. It seemed to take forever to reach the door, but eventually she got there and turned the doorknob. The door squeaked on its hinges as she pulled it open, making her teeth clench and sending a chill down her spine.

"Don't forget to feed the beast," said Dad.

Justine looked back at him and scowled. He grinned back, a cheery, sarcastic little smile that irritated her, as much for the fact that he was amused as for the knowledge that she should be as well.

Justine tried to smile back at him, then she turned, squared her shoulders, flipped on the light, and set off downstairs.

The steps down to the basement were plain slats of wood nailed to a simple support structure. There was no handrail. A single bulb, set into the basement ceiling in a fixture that was missing its cover, cast a dim glow that left the corners of the unfinished room in mysterious shadows. The air was filled with the odor of moisture and mildew beneath the scent of flowers from a plug-in air freshener that Mom had installed down there.

Justine reached the bottom of the stairs and stopped for a moment. Part of her screamed that she should just run back upstairs now, and let Mom deal with the stupid laundry. She stomped on that part of herself. She was beyond such silliness. Freshly determined, she turned to the left and walked toward the washer and dryer.

The two appliances sat against the far wall next to each other. A small table was set up to the right of the washer, where Mom would normally set the laundry basket. Detergent and dryer sheets sat on a shelf above the table. All was as it always was, but that was small comfort. Justine had always found the setup to be strangely disturbing, though she could never put her finger on why. It was probably just because it was in the basement, and the basement was creepy.

However she might tell herself that there was no reason to be scared, Justine still felt fear inching its way into her psyche as she approached the washer and dryer. The loading doors, set in the sides of the machines like closed mouths, seemed to almost grin at her with malicious glee.

Justine found herself throwing open the two doors with a force she did not intend. The washer's door opened more widely than normal and hit the dryer's with a metallic clang, stopping the dryer door from opening more than halfway. Justine blinked, then laughed into the back of her hand. She truly was being silly.

She shook her head, chiding herself for her childishness for the tenth time in the last two minutes, and set about moving the wet laundry from the washer into the dryer. It took less than a minute, all told. She shut the washer door and reached up to retrieve a dryer sheet from the shelf. As she pulled the sheet from its box, Justine looked down and saw two socks lying on the ground not far from the dryer.

Frowning, she bent down and examined them. They were a matched pair of argyle socks, the kind Dad liked to wear with his business suits. They were dry, the kind of dry that comes from the dryer, not from sitting out in the basement for a week. So she picked them up and shoved them into her pocket. Then she tossed the dryer sheet into the dryer, closed the door, and pushed the start button.

The dryer began its cycle and Justine turned away. Then she heard it. A low, drawling voice speaking from behind her.

"Justiiiiine."

Justine froze, fear - no, panic - flooding into her. She screamed at herself to run, get upstairs, but she could not move.

"Justiiiiine. Feeeeeed meeeee."

Then a scraping sound came from behind her and she sensed something moving.

Justine yelped and tried to run then, but her feet tangled up and she fell to the ground. Something cold touched the bottom of her foot and she wailed, pushing herself away. Tears streamed down her cheeks and she breathed in shallow gasps. What was it?

She looked behind her and froze in impotent terror.

The dryer had moved away from the wall toward her. It should have been straining against its power cord, but the cord stretched as though it was made on bungee. The machine itself had changed. It was no longer just a rectangular hunk of metal with a loading door in its front panel and controls on top. The two nobs on the control panel were sunken, darkened in their centers like the pupils on a pair of eyes. The loading door split in half horizontally and was partly open, revealing two rows of teeth. From the sides of the machine, two metallic protrusions, almost like arms, extended toward her, groping in the air as though reaching for something.

Justine opened her mouth to scream, but nothing came out. This had to be a dream!

"Justiiiiine. You know what I neeeed. Feeeeed meeeee."

The dryer monster came closer. Its mouth opened wider and she could see the gearing mechanism within the machine churning around behind the teeth almost like a hungry man licking his tongue over his lips.

A tiny squeak escaped Justine's lips and she pushed herself away as hard as she could. She managed to go three feet before she ran into something hard and narrow: the edge of the bottom-most stair. She scrambled around, clawing at the stairs until she managed to grab a handhold, then hauled herself to her feet and pushed herself upward toward the door, and safety.

Something round and metallic shot across the space in front of her, embedding itself into the wall with a solid THUNK. Justine's eyes widened as she realized what it was: the dryer monster's arm! Fairly gibbering with horror, she turned to find the dryer at the bottom of the stairs, its mouth gaping wide and its other arm plunged into the wall behind her, preventing her from moving in any direction.

"No," she begged weakly, her voice breaking as she backed into the wall and slumped down onto the stairs. "No, please." It was barely a whisper.

"I'm huuuungry. Feeeeed meeeee."

Justine sobbed again, tears flowing freely, and she hugged her knees close to her chest. She expected to feel the dryer monster's teeth sinking into her at any moment.

But then she felt a bulge in the side of her pants. What was that? She moved her hand to her pocket and she felt a flash of hope. The socks! What had Dad said about the socks?

Justine dug the socks out of her pocket and held them up in front of herself. The dryer monster's eyes narrowed and seemed to focus in on them.

"Yeeessssss. Feeeeed Meeeee."

The mouth opened wider than she imagined possible. Justine pressed herself back against the wall, trying to make herself flat so she could get away from the thing. Then she threw the two argyle socks into the dryer monster's mouth.

A deep sigh on contentment issued from the machine and its mouth closed. A low churning, different from its normal drying cycle, began to sound within it and the lines of its mouth turned up into a small smile. Then it retracted its arms from the wall on either side of Justine and retreated across the floor of the basement back to its place next to the washer.

Justine gasped in relief and slowly pushed herself to her feet. She wiped her eyes and her nose and stumbled her way up the stairs. She had just reached the door and was beginning to turn the doorknob when she heard the voice again.

"Justiiiiine."

She turned around slowly. And was struck in the face by something flying through the air at her. She batted at whatever it was and grabbed it. Her eyes widened when she saw what it was: a single argyle sock.

"Thaaaaank yooouuuu."

Justine shrieked and threw the door open. She burst into the living room and slammed the door shut, then sagged against it and slid to the floor. She wept, sobs of terror mixed with relief as adrenalin flowed through her body, making her skin tingle. She sat there for maybe half a minute before the crackling of folding paper from behind her caught her attention.

Justine turned her head to see Dad, still sitting at the table, looking over the fold of his newspaper with narrowed eyes and a small, knowing smile on his face.

"I told you so," he said.

BROTHER IN LAW, BROTHER IN BLOOD

The cityfolk stood in a wide semicircle around the edge of the bay, all eyes on the great pyre that workmen had been building for most of the previous week. Simply made, it had nonetheless been crafted with all the care a man puts into building his own home. For there, this night, they would light the fire of remembrance, to honor those who had gone before, and particularly those who had fought and died so that they could remain safe and free. They stood silently, the reverence of the occasion muting the natural conversations that would tend to crop up in a crowd of many hundreds.

Near the lapping waves of the bay, on the rightmost end of the circle, stood a man of medium height, with short-cut black hair and a closely trimmed beard that was broken by a scar that ran down the left side of his jaw. He wore well-cut clothing that was elegant in its simplicity, and a black furred cloak to ward off the early spring chill. At his side was a slender woman who stood perhaps a finger's breadth taller than he. She was blonde, beautiful, and dressed, as he was, simply but in clothing of obvious quality.

A small gap separated them from the other cityfolk, though as the couple looked at the people around them there was no animosity there; just an unspoken respect that bade the people given them some room, however unasked for the favor was.

At first the deference they showed him and Talia, after the Revolution, made Glover uncomfortable. He had tried to stop it, to make them realize that she and he were no different than they. That had any of them been in his or Talia's shoes during those terrible days, they would have made the same choices. But to no avail. They insisted on treating him like a hero, and her like the mother of liberty herself.

Never mind that the real hero was their brother.

At least Glover had been able to avoid being elected Mayor. Some damn fools wanted to rope him into that, despite his protests to the contrary. Fortunately, Higgins was more than happy to stand for election. Even more fortunately, he won.

Glover looked away from the pyre and the carved figures of the honored dead at its top, and found Higgins at the center of the semicircle, talking with the High Priest and making final preparations for the ceremony. As always for these sorts of events, Higgins wore the Mayor's purple frock and carried the rod of office cradled on his forearm and elbow. The High Priest, naturally, was clad in gold-trimmed white robes and carried a gnarled staff that was taller than he.

The pair nodded to each other, and the High Priest strode forward, toward the pyre. The crowd, already silent, somehow became even quieter. Even the babies at their mothers' breasts ceased their whimpers. For a long moment, as the holy man took his place before the pyre, the only sound was the lapping of the waves and the breeze in the trees, along with the buzzing of evening insects.

The High Priest turned to face the crowd and raised his hands above his head. "Brothers and Sisters," he intoned, "let us pray."

All bowed their heads, communing with the Creator silently in his or her own thoughts for a long moment. When they looked up, Mayor Higgins had joined the High Priest before the pyre.

"Fellow citizens," Higgins said in a deep voice that carried easily to the entire crowd, "on this, the sixth NewSpring since the Treaty, let us renew our resolve to remember our honored friends and family who went before, and the sacrifices they made so that we can now know peace, safety, and freedom. In this new era that they helped usher in, let us always remember the principles they fought and died for, and resolve to keep faith, that our children will not have to suffer as we did. Remember the honored dead. Long may their memory live."

"Long may it live," said the crowd in unison, the first words spoken by them in many minutes. Their united voices carried over the waters of the bay to the cliffs on the far side, and a few seconds later a more quiet, "Long may it live" echoed back as though the bay and the cliffs themselves had voiced their concurrence.

At the echo's return, the High Priest took his staff in both hands and tapped the ground at the base of two long-handled torches that were planted there for the ceremony. At his tapping, the torches sprang to light. Some in the crowd, newcomers to the region who had never participated in this ceremony before or some who just got caught up in things easily, gasped softly. Glover smiled in amusement; that was a simple trick involving the use of carefully prepared powders in the torches that reacted to a swift vibration. But if one did not know about the powder, it could almost appear the torches had been lit by magic.

Which was the point, of course.

Mayor Higgins and the High Priest each took up a torch and thrust it into the pyre. The wood had been carefully prepared, and it caught quickly. In a matter of moments the pyre was fully aflame, casting great light and heat which forced the crowd to move back several paces.

Mayor Higgins turned back to the crowd, smiling broadly. He made a gesture with both hands and, from behind the semicircle of citizens, bands began to play. "Citizens, eat and be happy. Enjoy the bounty that their sacrifice made possible."

On cue, the group took up a collective huzzah. Then the group began to split up. Some remained staring at the pyre for a time, consumed in their own thoughts. Many others turned and, talking amongst themselves with gradually increasing good cheer and boisterousness, made their way toward the bayside fairgrounds, where tables were laid out for all and food was prepared. Everyone had a hand in the preparing the food throughout the day of fasting leading up to the ceremony, so everyone had a claim to a meal, and was eager to partake.

Glover and Talia were among those who watched the pyre for a time. Hand-in-hand, they watched as the carved effigies representing the honored dead were consumed. And one in particular, larger than the others by a fair amount. Before it had caught fire, the effigy had been a powerful man whose face looked almost identical to Talia's.

She sniffed and took a kerchief from her pocket, dabbing at her eyes. "Grimly woulda been so embarrassed by this," she said.

Glover nodded, but smirked every so slightly. "He would have loved it all the same. You know how he liked attention."

"But not adoration."

Glover thought to object, but thinking on it for a moment decided Talia had the right of it. Her brother had been headstrong, always the first to fight but also always the first to laugh. He loved women and food and beer, and being the center of a party. But he shied away from accolades. One time he had actually hidden in the back of the stables to avoid being given an award from bravery.

That was just how he was.

"Come, love, let's get some food."

Talia nodded and, sliding her arm into Glover's, walked with him to the fairgrounds. There, Glover procured two plates of food. Talia took a bottle of wine and two cups. But they did not linger at the tables. Instead they left the fairgrounds and made their way up a small hill nearby. From there they had a commanding view of the fairgrounds, the pyre, and the bay, while also having a bit of privacy.

They sat down on the grass at the top and Glover set up their picnic, then they settled down to eat. They were silent for a while. Glover looked over at Talia and wondered at her melancholy. Most NewSpring nights she was jolly, but not this one. For whatever reason, she seemed to be feeling Grimly's loss almost as much as she had six years earlier.

"What do you suppose he would have thought of all this?"

Talia looked up at Glover, questioningly. "He always loved NewSpring."

"No. I mean, all this." Glover swept his hand over the bay, the fairgrounds, and toward the city, a mile distant. "How the world is now. Do you think he would approve?"

Talia frowned and sipped at her wine. "I think so. Didn't ye and him dream of a day when we would rule ourselves, not be ruled over by Lordlings whose only claim ta power was an accident of birth?"

Glover shrugged. "Not at first. You may recall I served one of those Lordlings, once upon a time."

Talia smiled broadly. "How can I forget. Ye were a sight ta see in yer armor. Swept me right off m' feet."

"And almost got my head cut off for it, too."

One of Talia's eyebrows quirked upward.

Glover felt himself flushing slightly, and he looked away. "Your brother...did not approve." She opened her mouth to object and he raised a calming hand to forestall her. "At first."

"I don't understand. Ye and Grimly were tighter than thieves. He loved ye like a brother."

Glover nodded. "And I him. Eventually."

Talia's lips pursed in that way they did when she was confused and was determined to figure out what had confused her, even if it took a month. For a second, Glover considered changing the subject, but he knew that look too well. He had planned to never tell her the story, but there was no getting out of it now.

He sighed. "Well, you recall when we were walking out together, he and I barely knew each other."

Talia nodded. "But ye became friends soon enough."

Glover looked at her askance. "We almost did not. Until the morning after your and my first full night together..." Talia flushed slightly, looking away girlishly. It was adorable how she still did that, even after all those years. Glover cleared his throat and continued. "Until that morning, he and I really had not said more than three sentences to each other. I'm pretty sure he knew you and I were together, but not that it was serious. You almost lost a husband that morning."

Talia's eyes widened in shock.

Glover spoke quickly so she would not interrupt the story before he could start it.

I stepped out of Madame Naulty's shop and smiled, bouncing my purchase in my hand for a moment before tucking it into my belt pouch. Last night with Talia had been wondrous, beyond my imaginings. Tonight promised to be even better. I tilted my face up into the early afternoon sunlight and breathed deeply. For a moment I lost myself completely in the glory of it all. The best girl in the city - Lord, in the country - had given herself to me, promised to be mine. Life simply could not be better. There was nothing that could bring me down, not today.

I stepped away from the shop and made my way through the crowded street toward the battlements, where I was due to take the watch in a quarter hour. Most people made way; my armor and sword, and Lord Tennebaum's coat of arms on my tabard, were enough to ensure that. All the same, it was slow going.

When I finally reached the steps leading up the city's inner wall, I only had a couple minutes before I had to take the watch. I took the steps two at a time and hurried toward the tower, not sparing a moment to look around. Which is why I didn't notice Grimly's presence until he called out to me.

"Hold it right there."

I stopped and turned around, knowing it was Grimly from his gravelly voice. I put on a smile of greeting, but it faded when I saw him. He wore the armor that his father had passed down to him: old, battered, but serviceable, and a scowl that would curdle milk. And he had his sword drawn, pointing at my face.

"Grimly," I said carefully, calmly. "Why so mad?"

Grimly just snarled and surged forward, drawing his sword back to attack. I took a step back and drew my own blade, and he stopped, his eyes narrowing cautiously despite the naked fury burning within them. My mind raced. We had not interacted very often, but things had always been cordial between us. Why...

"Talia did no come home last night." He practically spat the words out at me.

Oh no. This was not good. How had he learned what had happened? Talia did not live at home with him anymore, but with two other young ladyfriends. And ladyfriends talk. And talk gets around....

This was not good at all.

"I really think we ought to talk about this," I said.

"Nothin' ta talk about, ye bastehd," he said as he advanced again, stalking toward me with the grace of a fighting man, born and bred.

I, on the other hand, was newer at combat arms than he. I had seen him in the ring, and I was quite sure he was my better. And if I allowed this to actually turn into a fight, he would not be pulling his swings or striking for points. There was a very good chance I was about to lose my head.

I tried not to think on that as I slipped to the right and retreated, keeping him at a comfortable distance. Or at least a safe one.

"Sure there is."

He cut off my words with a swift attack, leaping forward and swinging his blade at my head. I managed to duck beneath it and retreated again, but the city wall was getting close now.

"Your sister is a jewel," I said between breaths.

That only enraged Grimly even more and he charged again, spittle flying.

"I would never dream of dishonoring her," I shouted as I leapt away again. I was almost too slow; his sword cut through my tabard and nicked off my breastplate before I got out of the way.

"Ye will no touch 'er again!" Grimly roared.

I continued backpedalling, but ran out of space as my back touched the crenellation atop the wall. There was only empty air behind me now until the moat, three dozen feet down. This was definitely bad.

But just then I could not have cared about that. Or the fact that Grimly was probably going to kill me. How dare he presume to dictate to me, or to Talia? I glared at him.

"I'd say that's her decision, not yours."

He snarled and wagged his sword at me. "Me Da's dead. 'Til she's wed, *I* say what happens wit 'er."

I flexed my fingers on the grip of my sword. Talia would never forgive me if I hurt him, assuming I could. Or him for hurting me. But...really Grimly?

I shook my head. "She's twenty-three years old, Grimly. Not like she's a maiden anymore."

I knew instantly that was the wrong thing to say. It was one thing to know that your little sister is a grown woman who has needs, and another thing to have someone else straight out tell you that she is no virgin. Especially when that person was the man you were ready to skewer for deflowering her.

Talia giggled. Really? He thought ye were my first?

I wasn't?

She rolled her eyes.

Grimly's eyes widened, his nostrils flared with rage, and he spat out a curse. "Shut yer mouth!" he screamed. And he charged straight at me full speed, his sword forgotten, as though to knock me over the wall.

It was either stand there and be crushed, skewer him as he came, or get out of the way.

I got out out of the way at the last possible instant, sidestepping to the right just before he hit me.

He struck the wall instead, face first, then fell to the floor.

For a moment I thought he had knocked himself out. Ot maybe knocked some sense into himself. But I was not that lucky. He shook his head groggily and pushed himself to his feet, then turned to face me again. His nose was bloodied and crooked; it was probably broken.

"Ye BASTEHD!" Grimly stalked forward again, his expression well past furious. Murder was in his eyes.

But for some reason I just could not help myself. I replied, deadpan, "I know who my father is. It's all legal and certified."

Grimly blinked and cocked his head to one side, looking at me as though I had said the strangest, most confusing thing in the world. I took advantage of his momentary pause to retreat along the wall toward the tower, putting more space between us.

"There's no reason we can't be brothers, you know."

I thought Grimly was enraged before; I was wrong. His face went positively beet red and he actually began to drool, he was so mad. What had I said?

"Yer da' did no touch me ma'!" he screamed, and charged again.

He did no think that!

That he did, my love. I loved him like a brother, but Good Lord he could be dense. Sometimes I'm not sure how he remembered to breathe.

Talia giggled again, nodding a reluctant agreement.

His statement took me completely by surprise. He almost skewered me before I remembered to back away again.

"I know that," I said in a rush. "I meant your sister."

One of Grimly's eyebrows quirked upward and I could tell he was confused again. "Huh?"

I glanced behind myself. I was running out of wall, but at least I was almost to the tower. Worst case, I could hide from him inside; maybe he would cool off during my watch. I readied myself for a dash to the tower door, but first gave talking one last try. "I meant how bout I marry your sister?"

Grimly stopped completely. He blinked. "Ye'd do that?"

I made a mental note not to tell Talia how incredulous he looked right then.

She laughed out loud. Was it that bad?

My love, you've no idea.

"Of course I would, you oaf. She agreed to it last night." I reached into my belt pouch with my left hand and pulled out the package I got from Madame Naulty. I held it out to him. "See?"

Grimly moved slowly, eyeing the package as though it were a venomous snake. Then he snatched it away, moving more quickly than I would have thought a man of his size could. He undid the tie and looked inside, and all the rage went out of him. He first looked dumbfounded, then a big silly grin spread on his face.

"Brother!" he cried, joyfully.

Next thing I knew he was crushing me in a great bear hug. I swear to God I thought I heard him sniffle. And sure enough, when he released me and stepped back, there were tears in the big lug's eyes.

"And that, my love, is how I got your brother's blessing for our marriage," Glover said. "And how he and I became friends."

Talia shook her head, still giggling. She ran her hand through her hair and the light from the pyre below glinted off the ring on her finger. The same simple silver band Glover bought that day at Madam Naulty's, along with its mate which he wore.

Talia stretched for a moment, and the flickering light accentuated the bulge in her belly where their child lay growing: Grimly, if a boy, or Yelena, after Glover's grandmother, if a girl. She then snuggled back against Glover's side. He pulled her close, and she leaned her head on his shoulder. Together they sat on the hilltop and looked down at the wide bay and the pyre at its edge, and they let the night's remembrances wash over them. After a time they stood and picked up their belongings, making ready to go home. Before they left, they said a prayer of thanks for the honored dead, but most of all for Grimly, a brother in blood, a brother in law. And a great man.

MESSAGE FROM THE AUTHOR

Thank you for reading my book. I hope you enjoyed reading it as much as I enjoyed writing it.

Every review helps an author out, so whether you loved this book, hated it, or something in between, please take a minute to tell other readers what you thought. All of the online retailers make it very easy to do, and I would really appreciate it.

Feel free to come say hi at my website or on Facebook. I always enjoy hearing from readers, especially since you all are, collectively, my boss.

I also have a weekly podcast, Story Time With Michael Kingswood, where I read stories and talk through some of the latest goings on in my world. I'd love to see you there.

Thanks again. My best to you and yours.

Warm Regards,
Michael Kingswood

MAILING LIST

If you enjoyed this book and would like word on new releases and special deals from Michael Kingswood, sign up for his newsletter on his website. Guaranteed to be spam-free, you can opt out at any time. And you can rest assured he will not share your information with anyone, for any reason.

https://michaelkingswood.com/newsletter-signup/

SUPPORTING PATRONAGE

Michael would like to invite you to become a supporting member of his website. Similar in concept to Patreon, a few dollars a month will give you access to exclusive content, and help him to focus more of his time to writing fun and exciting stories for your enjoyment.

Sign up at his website:

https://www.michaelkingswood.com/membership/supporting-patronage/

ABOUT THE AUTHOR

Michael Kingswood is 20-year veteran of the US Navy submarine force and a lifelong fan of science fiction and fantasy literature. His work has appeared in numerous collections and anthologies, to include the Fiction River Anthology series from WMG publishing. He holds a bachelors degree in Mechanical Engineering as well as a Master of Engineering Management and a Master of Business Administration. He has four children and currently resides in San Diego.

Find Michael Kingswood online at:

www.michaelkingswood.com

www.facebook.com/michael.kingswood

twitter.com/michaelkingswd

MORE BOOKS BY MICHAEL KINGSWOOD

GLIMMER VALE CHRONICLES

Glimmer Vale

Out-Dweller

Tollard's Peak

Robbed Blind

Wedding Gifts: A Glimmer Vale Chronicles Story

The Falconer's Stairs

Glimmer Vale Omnibus Edition #1

THE PERICLES CONSPIRACY

Passing In The Night

The Pericles Conspiracy

DAWN OF ENLIGHTENMENT

Masters Of The Sun

NOVELLAS

What Lurks Between

The Necromancer's Lair

The Champion

Veritas Morte

STORY COLLECTIONS

Tales Of Adventure #1

Tales Of Adventure #2

Short Story 10-Pack

A Jar Of Mixed Treats

SHORT FICTION

Michael has also published a number of shorter works, links to which can be found on his website.